DON'T MARRY HIM

by

J. Sterling

DON'T MARRY HIM

Edited by:

Jovana Shirley

Unforeseen Editing

www.unforeseenediting.com

Cover Design by:

Michelle Preast

www.Michelle-Preast.com

www.facebook.com/IndieBookCovers

ISBN: 978-1-945042-66-9

Please visit the author's website

www.j-sterling.com

to find out where additional versions may be purchased.

Thank you for purchasing this book.

I hope you enjoy my Fun for the Holidays collection!

Sign up for my newsletter to get emails about new releases, upcoming releases, and special price promotions:

NEWSLETTER

Come join my private reader group on Facebook for giveaways:

PRIVATE READER GROUP

facebook.com/groups/ThePerfectGameChangerGroup

Other Books by J. Sterling

Bitter Rivals—an enemies-to-lovers romance

Dear Heart, I Hate You

In Dreams—a new adult college romance

Chance Encounters—a coming-of-age story

THE GAME SERIES

The Perfect Game—Book One

The Game Changer—Book Two

The Sweetest Game—Book Three

The Other Game (Dean Carter)—Book Four

THE PLAYBOY SERIAL

Avoiding the Playboy—Episode #1

Resisting the Playboy—Episode #2

Wanting the Playboy—Episode #3

THE CELEBRITY SERIES

Seeing Stars—Madison & Walker

Breaking Stars—Paige & Tatum

Losing Stars—Quinn & Ryson

THE FISHER BROTHERS SERIES

No Bad Days—a new adult, second-chance romance

Guy Hater—an emotional love story

Adios Pantalones—a single-mom romance

Happy Ending

THE BOYS OF BASEBALL

(THE NEXT GENERATION OF FULLTON STATE BASEBALL PLAYERS)

The Ninth Inning—Cole Anders

Behind the Plate—Chance Carter

Safe at First—Mac Davies

FUN FOR THE HOLIDAYS

(A COLLECTION OF STAND-ALONE NOVELS WITH HOLIDAY-BASED THEMES)

Kissing My Coworker

Dumped for Valentine's

My Week with the Prince

Fools in Love

Spring's Second Chance

Don't Marry Him

Summer Lovin'

Flirting with Sunshine

Falling for the Boss

Tricked by My Ex

The Thanksgiving Hookup

Christmas with Saint

CROSSING LINES

DOMINIC

"YOU WANT ME to object at your wedding?" I asked again, simply for clarification. I knew that I'd heard her right the first time, but I wanted to hear her say it one more time … to make this fucking insane request of me again.

I'd been in love with Dove Tryst my entire life, and there was very little that I wouldn't do for the woman. We'd made it a habit to push each other's buttons, each of us doing some pretty insane shit for the other in the name of love—and sometimes hate—but this … this was going too far.

Even for us.

She stared at me silently, her green eyes daring me to tell her no as the wind whipped her blonde hair around.

"Dove, I haven't talked to you in months, and this is what you say to me after all this time? No explanations, no answers. Just this fucked up request after I find out you're marrying *him*?"

Silence.

It gave me time to take her in, to really look at her. I had this woman memorized, knew every inch of her by heart. I could recognize her in a lineup if I was blindfolded, just by the way her body felt underneath my fingertips. There were subtle changes that most men wouldn't notice, but I wasn't most men. Her blonde hair was longer than she normally kept it, falling past her full breasts instead of stopping just short of them. And her body was a shade darker and toned to a level she'd never been before. No doubt she'd been working out and getting in shape for her upcoming nuptials.

The perfect-looking bride.

Bile threatened to rise. I had never once entertained the idea that Dove would marry someone who wasn't me. It was absolutely fucking preposterous. My anger flared, betrayal and loathing filling me before flitting away with my next breath. I had a hard time staying angry with her.

Getting worked up was easy, but staying that way always eluded me.

Unlike her.

Dove could hold a grudge like no other. Whenever she got a little too pissed, it was me who ended up on his knees, asking for forgiveness. She gave it. For me, she'd claimed, she'd always give in. But now, here we were, standing in silence in the middle of some empty field in the town we'd both grown up in, a huge pear-shaped diamond on her ring finger that I hadn't given her.

"First, you break my fucking heart by getting engaged to him, of all people, and now, you want me to object at your goddamn wedding? A wedding I have no intention of showing up to, by the way."

More silence.

"As if I could stand there and watch you marry someone else—anyone else—and not die from the pain."

She was still quiet. And no tears fell. I'd expected at least some moisture to start forming at the corners of her eyes with my confessions, but there was nothing there.

Only hardness remained.

It was unnerving, her looking at me this way. My girl

was definitely fighting something internally, but I wasn't sure exactly what. This woman, who I knew as well as I knew myself, suddenly felt like a complete stranger. Nothing made sense.

"Fucking hell! Answer me, Dove!"

"Yes," she screamed back, losing all of her composure.

I found myself momentarily satisfied at her lack of control. Her anger, or irritation, or whatever it was meant that she still felt something for me. I hadn't lost her forever. There was still part of my girl in there, no matter how deep she tried to bury it and act like she didn't need me anymore.

We both knew that nothing could be further from the truth. One of us didn't exist without the other. There was only the two of us, and the whole damn town knew it. Which was why none of this made any kind of sense.

"I need you to object," she said, her voice more stoic now.

I shifted my weight from foot to foot, wrestling with what she was asking me to do. And for a reason she refused to give me.

"This is too much."

"I figured that you, of anyone else in the world, would relish in the chance to humiliate Trevor O'Connor in front of the whole town, all of his donors and constituents. Imagine how embarrassed he'd be if you not only stopped his wedding, but also ran off with the bride."

It was tempting.

Damn, it was *really* tempting.

Trevor used to be my best friend when we were younger. He'd had a fucked-up home life. A dad who struggled to stay sober and a mom who rarely, if ever, came back to the run-down two-bedroom apartment they called home. He moved into our mansion as soon as my father gave me the okay. He even had his own room. I thought I was doing the right thing at the time, helping out a friend in need. I never realized that he'd turn into my biggest threat.

I learned in that moment what it was like to be competed with—for my father's attention, for accolades, for jobs, and for girls. Trevor wanted everything that I had, and with the exception of Dove, I happily handed it all over to him. Nothing, except her, meant anything to me.

He followed in my father's footsteps, learning the ins

and outs of the political circuit. Trevor fed off of the manipulation and power—two things I'd always steered clear of, much to both of my parents' ire. I had no desire to be the type of man my father was or to follow in the family business. I came from a long line of politicians, where nothing was off the table when it came to getting what you wanted.

Dove was the one thing that I kept for myself. She was never a bargaining chip, never an option on anyone's agenda. She had been mine, end of story, and everyone had fucking known it. But now, somehow, she was his, and nothing made sense anymore.

So, yeah, it was tempting as fuck to want to steal her from right under his nose on what was supposed to be the happiest day of his life. But I had to think straight. And while the idea that Dove had planted in my head was a good one, it wasn't necessarily smart.

My jaw ticced as I looked at her, forcing my hands to stay put and not reach for her like they were so used to doing. She was waiting for my response.

"If I did that …" I swallowed hard, searching my mind for a time I'd ever turned her down. I couldn't think of one. "If I stopped the wedding and you left him at the altar, Trevor would be the victim. Everyone would feel sorry for him. Hell, it would probably get him more votes and reach, not less. He'd be some sort of hero to the everyday people. His next campaign slogan or some shit. And we'd be the villains, Dove. In that scenario, you and I? We'd be the bad guys. The entire town would hate us. Everything we'd worked for would go under, like *that.*" I snapped my fingers to signal how quickly we'd lose it all. "No one would support our businesses; they wouldn't be allowed to without scandal following them at every turn. People would be forced to choose a side, and they wouldn't choose ours."

Not that I honestly gave a shit about my development company. I could always start over online or somewhere else. And it wasn't that I needed the money. I had plenty from my success over the years, saved up and accruing nicely regardless of the economy. And I knew that Dove had her finances in check too. She'd bought Hopetown Real Estate and turned it into the most successful residential company in the county, not just the city limits. It had taken her years to turn the business around and make it into what it was today. I couldn't imagine her walking away from it like it wouldn't break her heart to do it.

If the town turned on us, I knew it would devastate her. She loved it here in Hopetown as much as I hated it. I never planned on leaving though because Dove never wanted to. Even though corruption ran through the neighborhoods like telephone wires, Hopetown would always be home. It was where she wanted to raise our family, and I never planned on denying her that.

I hadn't expected her face to look so crestfallen with my words, but that was exactly what happened. She looked like she was about to break. The tears I'd wanted to see a few minutes ago now appeared. I didn't want them now. I'd wanted them then. Now, they made me feel like an asshole. Now, they made me question more than ever what the hell was really going on that she wasn't telling me.

"Can you really stand the thought of me being someone else's wife? Of being *his* wife? I thought we were soul mates, Dominic. I thought you loved me."

My cheek stung with the force of her words like she had slapped me with them. And watching her walk away had almost been as bad as being struck.

"How could you do this? You owe me an explanation, Dove!" I shouted, and she stopped moving. "Why the hell did you say yes to him?"

"You're joking, right?" was the answer she gave me, and I wanted to tear my fucking hair out piece by piece as she climbed into her all-white Range Rover.

That wasn't a fucking answer.

Dove drove off anyway, the loose gravel from the road spitting up behind her tires and flying toward me. A piece hit the sunglasses on top of my head, leaving a mark. It seemed fitting that something else besides me would carry the scars from today's meeting.

I kicked the gravel with my boot, sending dirt and debris into the air.

She thought I loved her. I thought she loved me. Even when she acted like she hated me, I knew she still loved me. But marrying someone else wasn't love. It was punishment. It was torture. It was downright fucking cruel. Yet she was doing it.

My heart split in half inside my chest. It hurt almost as bad as it had the day I found out that she was engaged to *him*. The day my world stopped turning and life hit the pause button.

Moving forward, without her, seemed impossible.

I stopped talking to my family the minute I caught wind of the news. There was no way they hadn't been in on this soul-level deception, and I knew it without even having to ask. I wondered how long they had been plotting it, how long this treachery had been in the works behind my back.

My father knew exactly how badly losing Dove would gut me. He knew she was my Achilles heel, the person I couldn't function without. That was the thing about the people closest to you—the moment they knew your weaknesses, they wouldn't hesitate to exploit them when necessary. My father would do whatever it took to get whatever he needed even if I had no earthly idea what that was. Apparently, he'd needed me out of the way and Dove by Trevor's side.

But why? I wondered as more questions than answers filled my head.

All to climb the political ladder? It didn't make sense.

And how had they gotten Dove to agree? She loathed

Trevor as much as I did. Her loyalty had never strayed from me. Until now.

I had a choice to make. But when it came to Dove, there was never truly a choice. I'd do anything that woman asked, and we both knew it.

But objecting at a wedding she'd willingly agreed to be a part of?

That was definitely crossing a line, yet she'd asked for it anyway. I replayed her words in my head, and that was when I caught her slipup. A rarity for Dove. Unless it was done on purpose, which was more than likely the case.

What was she trying to tell me that she couldn't come right out and say?

"I need you to object," she had told me.

Need.

Not want.

She *needed* me to do this. And we both knew that I would.

PUSHED TOO FAR

DOVE

I DROVE AWAY, my heart bleeding out in his hands and he didn't even realize it. Dominic DeLuca was convinced this was some sort of game that I was playing. I had seen it in his dark eyes—the questioning, the hesitation, the uncertainty of what I was asking him to do without telling him why.

But Dominic, of all people, should have realized that if I was leaving information out, there was a damn good reason for it. I couldn't tell him anything without Trevor finding out about it and doing what he'd threatened. I'd promised that I'd marry him, be a good little wife, and play the part for as long as I had to. I was determined to eventually find a way out of this charade. But for now, it was the only way to keep my dad from going to prison. I knew what people in jail did to the cops who ended up there. If there was any way I could stop that from happening, I had to do it.

Being in Dominic's presence, sharing the same air, had almost made me pass out. It was unnatural to be that close to him and not touch him. My body wanted to move to its rightful place—in his arms—but my brain refused to allow it. I had to be strong. He had known what he was doing when he came to meet me—dressed in my favorite navy-blue suit, looking stunning with his dark hair gelled back to perfection and the beard on his face perfectly trimmed.

I'd loved that man my whole life. How was I supposed to live without him?

Dominic and I had a history of pushing too far. We'd tested limits and boundaries, all in the name of love, asking some pretty questionable things of the other. All of that was mostly in the past though. We had been young when we first fell in love, first became each other's everything, and realized that this was what books, movies, and TV shows always talked about. Other halves. People you couldn't live without. A partner who would fight through the pits of hell to be by your side and never let go.

I believed in soul mates because I'd found mine. And I had constantly made him prove it. I was insecure in the beginning, unsure that a guy as cool and confident as Dominic could feel for me the way I felt for him, so my asks usually involved other girls. They wanted him. He was mine. He let them know they'd never have a chance in the most humiliating way possible. I asked him for cruelty. He delivered.

I could be petty and immature. Dominic never scolded me for it though. Not the way I did to myself when I was alone at night, torn between feeling elated that he could wield such harshness in my honor and hating myself for asking him to do it.

I knew for a fact that there was no other soul on earth who would do the things that Dominic did for me. And in return, when he asked me for the same proof of loyalty, I never hesitated. We were always making each other walk through fire.

We both knew how screwed up we were acting back in those days, actually talked about it a lot, but we couldn't seem to help ourselves. I'd grown addicted to making him jump through hoops to prove his devotion. I craved his attention, needed it to survive at times.

And Dominic … he would do anything I asked, just to keep me happy … and *his*. He wanted something that belonged to him, something he didn't ever have to share with anyone else, and I was all too willing to be exactly that.

Growing up in a household filled with betrayal and lies did that to a person. Once Dominic was old enough to figure out how the political games worked, he started questioning every single thing he'd ever been told. Where did the spinning of stories end? Not in the sanctity of home, like I had naively told him one time when we were younger. No, a story got spun twenty-four hours a day, three hundred sixty-five days a year if that was what needed to happen. It didn't matter who was lied to. All that mattered was that the right people believed the lies. And then did what they were told. Not to mention, kept their mouths shut.

It didn't occur to me that the people you were supposed to trust the most, like parents, could be the biggest deceivers. That fact only further cemented my and Dominic's connection. He couldn't trust anyone, except me. He was growing up in a house where he felt like a pawn in a game he didn't want to play. His parents both tried to mold him into the perfect future politician even though he didn't want it. Every time he tried to rebel, he was punished and told it was for his own good.

He'd made me promise that I'd never lie to him and never leave him.

I always did as he'd asked … until today.

My dad, on the other hand, was one of the good guys. Or at least, he tried to be.

I'd overheard someone in our home one night during my freshman year of high school, offering my dad a bribe of some kind. I didn't really get what they were asking, but I understood what they wanted my father to do. He needed to look the other way and arrive late to a call, giving the man enough time to get away without being caught. Being the chief of police who respected the badge and a stand-up guy with integrity, he told them no. At first.

Then, I heard the man mention my name.

And then say something about my mom.

She'd died when I was just a toddler. An unfortunate car accident—or so I'd been told. I had even been in the car at the time but was somehow spared. I started wondering if it hadn't been an *accident* at all and hoped that wasn't the case even though I'd heard rumors to the contrary over the years, mentioning the Firenzi family.

My dad's voice rose, his tone angry. He didn't like being blackmailed, and he said as much, his fist punching the wood table in frustration.

He gave in that night, telling the man that this wouldn't become a habit—the asking for favors by threatening what he held dear.

Once he opens that door, how the hell is he ever supposed to close it again? I wondered, and Dominic asked the same thing after I told him what happened.

I watched my dad take an envelope filled with money before tossing it on the floor, the bills spilling out. And I knew he'd only done it to protect me because I'd been threatened somehow. He tried so hard to be good, but even a righteous man caved when the people he loved were on the line.

Even as a teenager, I understood his betrayal in that moment and didn't hate him for it. I couldn't. I loved my dad and knew that he'd do anything to keep me safe. But that night, something inside me had shifted ever so slightly. I never looked at people quite the same way again.

When someone you trusted implicitly could do the wrong thing, no matter the reasoning, it changed the way you saw the world. And knowing that others would use and manipulate for their own personal gain scared me in a way I'd never really considered before. It was one thing when Dominic talked about it, but it was another to witness it firsthand. But the most shocking realization for me was recognizing where my own weaknesses lay if the tables were ever turned against me.

After that evening, Dominic and I had created a world where only the two of us existed. A secret fantasy of a place, where we were never let down, lied to, or betrayed in any way. There was only love. Which was how I'd gotten into this mess in the first place. It was so obvious now. When you lived your life blind to anyone else in it, it was easy to get stabbed in the back. You never saw it coming until it was too late and the damage had been done.

Dominic had to know that I'd never in a million years

willingly marry anyone who wasn't him, especially Trevor O'Connor. How could he not know at least that? After all this time, my love for him should be the one thing he never questioned.

But then again, I'd been keeping secrets and lying to him since the day I'd been forced to break up with him without reason all those months ago. The promises that had meant the most to him—for me to never lie or leave him—were shot to hell. Trevor would stop at nothing to hurt Dominic, and using me was the perfect way to do it.

Trevor had always wanted me, ever since high school. He'd told me a million times over the years, joking at first—before his *jokes* turned more serious. I never thought there was a world in which someone taking me from Dominic could happen. I was off-limits. Unattainable. Not up for grabs. And anyone who didn't realize that usually got a rude awakening to that fact real quick. I belonged to Dominic DeLuca and always would regardless of our relationship status at the time.

Dominic and I convinced ourselves that Trevor's obsession with me didn't matter, that he would eventually get bored and find someone new to focus on. Over the years, he dated other women, but they always had one thing in common—they looked a little too much like me. We should have known better … been smarter. Men like Trevor didn't like to lose and would go to extreme measures to get what they wanted. No lengths were too far as long as their ego was satiated. I'd been wounding Trevor's pride for long enough.

Which was why I knew that Dominic would eventually forgive me once he learned the truth. Forgiving each other would be easy. Because the idea of not doing it was unthinkable. Things had gotten so out of control between us, so fast. I had been forced to break up with Dominic, and the next thing I knew, I was on the arm of a man I hated, pretending to be his proud and doting girlfriend as he announced his run for office. Every face I saw wore the same expression as I stood there with Trevor—utter confusion.

I had been given a choice all those months ago, but there really hadn't been one. I'd do anything to keep my dad safe, and Trevor and Dominic's father both knew it. Yes, Dominic's father was in on this as well. Something about me being the perfect politician's wife. He'd said it to me before in the past, but I'd thought he always meant as long as I was with Dominic. Apparently, the husband part was interchangeable. I, however, was not.

When I'd first texted Dominic and asked him to meet me in the middle of an empty field, far from prying eyes, I hadn't intended on asking anything of him, especially not something so reckless. I just wanted to see him even if I couldn't give him an explanation or any of the answers that he deserved. I'd been dying inside without him. We'd never gone more than twenty-four hours without speaking before, and now, I'd been ignoring his texts and calls for months. It was the only way I could ever go through with this.

"I need you to object," had tumbled out of my mouth without warning, and my entire body froze.

I hadn't meant to say it.

I hadn't meant to say anything.

Staying quiet while he'd hurled accusations at me was damn near impossible, but I'd done it until he pushed too hard, forcing my composure to crumble.

Then, I went back to the original ask. I'd started to convince myself it was a brilliant idea even though I should have known better.

Dominic objecting during the ceremony felt like some sort of reasonable loophole. Trevor couldn't get mad at me because I wouldn't have done anything wrong. I'd have shown up like he'd asked—dressed in all white with a smile on my face. I couldn't have foreseen what Dominic would do. He could be rash, angry, and unstable. Especially when I was involved.

I'd tell Trevor that I only ran outside with Dominic to calm him down, to force him to leave, and to convince him that I didn't want him anymore.

I rolled it all around in my head as I headed back into town, knowing damn well that there was no way in hell that Trevor would believe any of it. He'd had a front row seat to our relationship for far too many years. He knew the way Dominic and I worked.

I'd been an idiot to ask Dominic something so stupid without thinking about it from every angle first. It wasn't like me to be so rash, especially when my dad's future was on the line. My only excuse was that seeing Dominic had rendered me unable to think clearly. And now, the damage had been done.

I'd planted a seed in Dominic's head that I needed to get out. But how the hell was I going to accomplish that without telling him everything?

I needed to think of something—and fast. I was running out of time.

I DON'T UNDERSTAND

DOMINIC

I'D BEEN RATTLED ever since I'd met with Dove earlier this morning. So, now, in my favorite diner, I was sitting on an aging booth with cracks in the leather backrest. Across from me was my best friend, Michael. He had solidified his place as my only friend outside of Dove in our junior year of high school when he informed me that Trevor was scheming to take my girl from me. I laughed at the time, knowing that there was nothing anyone on this fucking planet could do to take her from my arms, but the fact that Trevor was going behind my back to truly attempt something like that? The betrayal had me seeing red.

Michael didn't know the specifics, only that Trevor was willing to stop at nothing to have her. He'd overheard him talking in the locker room with some guys. Trevor had always been obsessed with Dove, but I chalked it up to just another one of those things that I had that Trevor coveted. I'd been used to it by then. Him wanting Dove didn't surprise me one bit. Every guy at our school wished they were me. But no one was stupid enough to do anything about it.

It wasn't until I replayed a conversation between myself and my father that it all started to make sense. My father loved Dove. And I mean, he saw her as the perfect woman to have on my arm as I ran for city mayor before eventually running for bigger and better positions within our fair state. Two things I never intended on doing, no matter how hard he pushed and plotted.

Dove was the daughter of a well-respected pillar of our community. Her father was the chief of police and *having a man like that on our side was crucial to being successful and navigating certain waters of our town and the perimeter. The union couldn't have been more perfect if it had been arranged by our forefathers.* That was what he had told me one uncharacteristically hot and sunny afternoon in December. That I'd done well for myself, securing Dove, and he'd been proud of my choice.

Looking back, I thought that was the last time my dad had said those words to me. That he had been proud.

"Are you listening, man?" Michael snapped his fingers in front of my face, and I swatted them away.

"Sorry. Out of it," I admitted, and he groaned.

"Are you going to tell me what happened with Dove, or are you going to just sit here all day long, looking like someone kicked your dog?"

Glancing around the crowded diner, I leaned toward Michael and away from any potentially prying ears. People in Hopetown were always listening. Especially now.

"She asked me to stop the wedding," I all but whispered.

"She what?" the dumbass shouted.

"Keep your voice down," I growled.

Michael leaned back and watched me. Crossing his arms over his chest, he cocked his head as a wide grin emerged. "You're gonna do it, aren't you?"

I looked around again to make sure there were no eyes on us. "Of course, I'm going to do it. What do you expect? It's Dove."

"I always knew that woman was going to get you into

trouble someday." He instantly moved forward, his arms on the tabletop as he stared at me.

I shook my head. "Something's not right about any of this."

"No shit, brother. There's nothing right about Dove marrying someone who isn't you," he said before taking a gulp of his coffee. "It doesn't make sense. Have you thought about all the possibilities?"

"What are you saying exactly?" I pushed because I didn't trust my own interpretation of things. I was too jaded; I couldn't see clearly. I no longer trusted my gut in this situation.

"Dove would *never* do this." He emphasized the word *never*. "Not without a reason."

My eyes shot up to meet his, my head nodding in silent agreement. "What are you thinking?"

"That they have something on her." His answer was straightforward and to the point, and I wanted to laugh. "It's the only logical explanation."

"Like they're blackmailing her?" I asked almost incredulously. The idea seemed so far-fetched, like something out of a bad movie, but nothing else added up.

"Exactly."

I couldn't for the life of me figure out what would make Dove agree to do something as preposterous as marry Trevor. And while blackmail seemed like a somewhat-reasonable option, part of me didn't want to believe it.

"But how? She hasn't done anything wrong."

"What about you?"

"What do you mean, me?"

"Have you done anything that they could use against you? Get you in trouble somehow?" he asked before adding, "Dove would do anything to protect you."

"Shit," I breathed out, leaning back, looking straight up at the ceiling tiles as my mind raced.

There wasn't a single thing I could think of. I might have grown up with a manipulative politician for a father, but I mirrored myself after the man who had raised Dove. It was his integrity that I respected and wanted to be like.

"Is there something?" Michael asked, his tone more than a little curious.

I was sure, over the years, he'd wondered how our business had been so successful. When the economy took a hit, we never seemed to. There was stability in selling the kinds of things that people always needed.

I waved him off. "No. I've done everything by the book. I've never wanted anyone to be able to hold anything over my head." I'd been too smart for that, too aware of how things worked. "I've never asked anyone for any favors or special treatment."

"Then, what could it be? I mean, if it's not you, then—" he started to ask, and I cut him off.

"Who? If it's not me she's protecting, then who?"

"What are you thinking?"

"That there's only one other person on this planet she'd do anything for," I said before feeling a headache start to creep in between my eyes.

"We'd better go talk to Dove's dad then," he said matter-of-factly, as if he were a part of this now.

I laughed and put up a hand to stop him from exiting the booth. "You're not coming with me."

"The hell I'm not."

"Let me find out what's going on first." I rubbed my fingers above my eyes to try to ease the tension pooling there. "If I even can. Then, I'm going to need your help to stop this wedding."

He slapped his hands together and rubbed like a murderous mastermind. "I like the sound of that. I'm in."

I wanted to be annoyed at his overt excitement, but I was more than a little grateful for it instead. Going through this torment day in and day out was one thing, but having a friend who actually gave a shit made me feel less alone.

And I was going to need all the help I could get on Dove's wedding day.

SECRETS ARE THE WORST

DOVE

I PARKED MY Range Rover in front of the real estate office that I owned. Normally, I'd feel the surge of pride up and down my spine as I walked toward the front door. But today, like most days recently, I wanted to crawl into a hole and never come out. It used to be my sanctuary, and now, it felt soiled. A place where I'd relished in what I'd built and accomplished had turned sour.

I pulled open the glass door, and the air-conditioning hit me as I stepped inside. My best friend, Kristina, worked with me there, and her eyes met mine, narrowing as her smile turned into a frown.

"Your fiancé is waiting for you in your office." She made a gagging sound and put her finger down her throat.

Kristina had no idea what was really going on. She

didn't buy the engagement ruse at all, and her nonstop questions about it had grown tiresome. For whatever reason though, it was easier to hide the truth from her and eventually get her to back off and calm down. Dominic never would. Surely, Trevor had to know that.

I hated that he was here, in my space, where he didn't belong and never would. Walking through my office door, I plastered on a fake smile and sat down at my desk—as far away from him as possible.

"Where were you?" Trevor closed the door shut with one arm before leaning his body forward, inching toward me.

"Looking at a property. Why?"

"Don't lie to me, Dove," he growled, and I imagined picking up a chair, tossing it at his head, and watching him bleed out all over my floor.

"If you already know where I was, then why are you asking me?" I felt nerves course through my already-tense body.

I assumed Trevor had me followed at times, but I'd been careful today. No cars had tailed me. I'd made sure and checked the way my dad had taught me when I was just a teenager.

"You're not allowed to see him." His blue eyes narrowed into angry slits, and I hated that he truly believed he could control me. He pointed a finger at me. "Don't see Dom again. Don't talk to him. Don't text him. Don't call him. No more private fucking meetings someplace you think I won't know about. I. Know. Everything." His fists slammed on top of my desk, punctuating the last three words before he looked around to make sure no one in my office was watching him lose his composure.

My throat instantly dried up. "What are you talking about?"

Reaching for his cell phone, he typed quickly before spinning it around to face me. "Don't play stupid and don't act like I'm not always going to be ten steps ahead of you, sweetheart."

I squinted my eyes to try to read what was on it before realizing it was information about my phone—location, recent texts sent, and messages received. I should have known better. Trevor was deep in the political arena, so being able to infiltrate my phone shouldn't have surprised me, but for some reason, it still did.

If there were strings to be pulled, Trevor yanked on them. The second he left my office, I planned on heading down to the cell phone store to make sure my device couldn't be tracked like that. If he had put something on it, I'd have it taken off. If there was software available to block my phone from being accessed from the outside, I'd purchase it. I refused to lose my privacy that easily.

"What did you tell him, Dove? What did you tell Dom?" he pushed, and my mind raced, trying to think up an excuse that sounded plausible enough.

"Nothing. I didn't tell him anything," I said. It wasn't a lie.

"Then, why did you see him? Oh, right. Because the two of you can't live without each other." He mimicked a weak-sounding voice, clearly making fun of what Dominic and I shared. "Better start learning how or else he'll be the next to fall. You have no idea the amount of dirt I have on them. I've been planning this for years."

Threatening my dad had scared me half to death, but threatening Dominic filled my guts with pure, unadulterated rage. My jaw slid open with my surprise at his admission. Who the hell had the patience to plot something for so long? Someone with a vendetta, I imagined. And I genuinely believed that he had the power to go through with it, especially since when he had first told me about said dirt on my dad, he'd mentioned the person that my dad had taken the bribe from all those years ago. It wasn't out of the question that my dad had done it more than just that one time. It was probably more likely that he had than that he hadn't.

"He's been texting and calling me nonstop. I had to see him to tell him to back off."

"I highly doubt that." Trevor knew better.

He leaned even further across my desk in some feeble attempt to close the space between us, but my body pulled away in response. He laughed at my discomfort. It was like it brought him joy in some sick and twisted way.

Forcing myself to calm down, I took a deep breath and blew it out slowly. "What more do you want from me, Trevor? I've agreed to marry you, and I will. I've kept my mouth shut, which I will also continue doing. All of this is going to destroy Dominic, and I know that's all you really want anyway."

His features curled as a smug smile appeared across his

face. "You're not wrong."

I shook my head. I'd never been able to get him to admit that this whole charade was about Dominic even though I knew it had to be. He'd always alluded that ruining Dominic was only part of the reason, but now, I was actually getting somewhere.

"All of this is just to hurt Dominic? Why?"

Trevor looked almost relieved that I'd finally asked, and he launched into some sort of maniacal diatribe. "Because he has everything without even trying! The last name. The power. Money. You. He hasn't had to work for anything! Everything just falls into his lap, and the whole town worships him for it. I'm sick of being in his shadow. It's time the town saw me as a winner instead of second best to the golden boy who doesn't even want the title!"

I wanted to argue because Dominic had started his business without any help and made it into what it was today all on his own. He'd never used his name for clout, refused to fall in line and do what was expected of him. If anything, he'd made his life so much harder by going against his father's wishes.

"He looked out for you. Brought you home, so you

could have a better life."

Trevor made a disgusted sound as spit flew from his lips. "He pitied me. He's always pitied me."

"That's not true."

At least, it hadn't been at the start. Dominic had genuinely liked Trevor, trusted him even. But all that had changed sometime during high school.

"It doesn't matter," he challenged. "None of it matters now because I have you. So, you see, Dove, I win."

My stomach twisted into knots. I knew this was a game to him, but it seemed so fucking insane that the only reason behind all the conniving and manipulation was because he despised Dominic.

"You really hate him that much?"

He leveled me with a glare so vicious that it made my skin crawl. "I want him to know what it feels like to have nothing. To know how the misery can burn through the cells in your body every second of every day. To wake up each morning filled with dread instead of hope and knowing there's no way out of it. He's never experienced a single day like that. Now, he'll live a whole lifetime of it."

Trevor sounded so proud of what he'd been able to

accomplish—blackmailing me into leaving the only man I'd ever loved.

"You know I'll never love you, right? This will never be real," I asked, my voice coming out in a broken whisper as he sat down and crossed his legs. He looked so relaxed and in control, while I felt completely out of it.

"Yes, Dove, I know you'll never love me. The thing is, I don't care. This isn't about love. Knowing that Dominic will never be happy again is all that matters to me. I want to destroy him."

"You really are vile," I said, my tone louder this time.

"Don't sound so surprised, sweetheart."

But I was. I truly was. Knowing that Trevor felt competitive was one thing, normal even, but this was on a completely different level. This went beyond typical guy-ego stuff.

"Oh yeah, if you are even thinking about planning something disruptive during our wedding, you'd better stop now. There is no scheme that the two of you could come up with that I haven't already anticipated. So, if I were you, I'd call Dominic off, or I'll have your dad arrested during our reception. In front of everyone. And you and I will both stand there and watch him get hauled off in the back of a cop car. Are we clear?"

If I'd thought my throat had dried up before, it was the Sahara Desert now. I almost started choking. I couldn't breathe. I despised feeling weak and powerless, and somehow, Trevor excelled at making me feel both.

"There are no plans," I attempted to say, but the words got caught, and I started coughing. Thank God there was a glass of water on my desk. I downed the entire thing in one long gulp. My eyes met Trevor's as I repeated the last line. "There are no plans. Nothing is happening."

"Keep it that way," he demanded before shoving the chair back and standing to leave. "Don't forget about dinner tonight. I'll have a car pick you up at seven. Wear the black Chanel."

I watched him walk out the door before I lost it completely. A hundred different ways of bashing his brains in flashed through my mind.

If only I wouldn't go to prison after doing it, I thought to myself.

Dominic had never controlled me. It was such a foreign feeling—being told what to do at every turn. How to dress. How to speak. How to act appropriately. I wasn't usually the type to acquiesce, but this wasn't a normal situation I'd gotten myself into.

Kristina walked into my office, her dark hair swishing across her shoulders, distracting me from my own self-hatred. "I can't stand that you're engaged to that prick. But I hate more that you won't tell me why or what happened between you and Dom."

She was starting in again, and I was in no frame of mind to deal with her nonstop questions.

"Just stop. Please." It was all I could manage at the moment.

Seeing Dominic earlier had drained me. Listening to Trevor's threats had only further deflated me. My head was still spinning from the fact that he had been able to get into my phone this whole time and I'd been too stupid to realize it.

"I'm just saying, you understand that no one buys this, right? Not a single person in this entire town thinks that you love Trevor O'Connor."

I wanted to throw up, but I steeled myself and looked right at my best friend as I delivered a single word that I knew would tell her everything she needed to know without actually admitting anything. "Good."

"I knew it." She started shaking her head as her features hardened. Kristina had always been a fiercely loyal friend, and I loved her for it. "You have to let me help you."

"I can't," I said before my resilience started to fade. I got nervous that she might accidentally slip and say something in front of the wrong person, and everything I'd worked hard to save would fall apart. "Trust me, if there was something you could do, I'd let you. But there's nothing. And you can't say anything, Kristina. I mean it. Not to anyone."

"Not even Dom?"

"Especially not Dominic, said, emphasizing his name. I'd already awoken that particular beast, and I needed to figure out how to put him back to bed.

"What about your dad?"

"Not him either. Promise me you won't say a word."

"I don't even have anything to say."

"I need you to promise," I pushed.

She looked at me before locking her lips with her

fingers and tossing the key. "I promise. But I don't like it. Not one bit. Just for the record."

"Neither do I."

WE HAVE TO SAVE HER

DOMINIC

I LEFT THE diner and drove straight to the police station without so much as a plan or any inkling of what I was going to say to Dove's dad.

The chief of police hadn't always been my biggest fan, but I soon realized that it wasn't me he despised as much as it was the family I came from. He tried his best to separate who I was from my father, but I could see how much he struggled with it … especially in the beginning, when I spent more time at his house than my own.

Once he realized that I wasn't going anywhere and that Dove and I were absolutely mad for each other, he took the time to get to know me better. I modeled myself after him, wanted to be the kind of man that he was rather than the one who had raised me.

Bob Tryst took me in, and the person who used to look at me with disdain every time he saw me started looking at me like I was family. I had no idea how he'd look at me now.

Sauntering up to the reception desk, I smiled at Sarina, a woman I'd known since she moved into town.

"Well, well, well. What brings you in here, sugar?"

I couldn't help but laugh as she fussed with her graying hair, pretending to make herself presentable for me.

"Just came to see you," I teased, and her cheeks instantly blushed.

"Stop it. You're going to give an old woman a heart attack." She tapped her acrylic nails on top of the counter, one at a time.

"I came to see Bob. Is he here?"

"Sure, honey. He's in the back. Just sign in, and I'll ring him," she said as she pushed a clipboard toward me to fill out.

I grabbed the pen and signed my name before looking at the wall for the time and adding it on the next line. My stomach turned when I realized that I had no idea what I was going to say to him. What if he was happy about the wedding? It never occurred to me that he might be on board with it.

I closed my eyes tight. Sarina cleared her throat, and I opened them, remembering that I wasn't alone.

"Didn't want to interrupt whatever war you were battling in there." She tapped on the side of her head, her expression sad. "He's waiting for you."

"Thanks," I said, and she let me walk away without another word.

I was grateful she hadn't mentioned Dove or the upcoming wedding or else I might have broken down in the middle of the hallway.

The door buzzed as I approached it, signaling that it was unlocked, and I pulled it open and stepped through another set of doors and into the "war room," as the cops called it. There were desks and whiteboards with cases being worked on. My eyes scanned over some of the writing, stopping on an entire oversize board devoted to the Firenzi organization, complete with photographs and flow charts.

They were a family here in town with ties to the mob.

Everyone knew it, but no one apparently knew how to prove it. Anyone who got too close ended up either missing or dead. It wasn't hard to figure out who'd done it, but they were incredibly clever at covering their tracks. No one had been able to hold them in jail for longer than twenty-four hours. There was never enough evidence against them. At least, not the kind that was sticky enough to hold up in court.

Bob suddenly appeared in front of me, a grim smile on his face. "Hey, son. It's been a while."

He extended his hand and shook mine harder than I'd expected before giving me a nod toward his office. I followed close behind him, avoiding the eyes in the room that were undoubtedly watching my every move. Everyone knew that Dove was engaged to Trevor, and I was sure it made about as much sense to them as it did to me.

"Still trying to bring down the Firenzi family, eh?" I said, hoping to break the ice.

His steps faltered for only a second before he gave me a curt nod. "Someone's always working that case. They're bound to screw up at some point."

Heading inside his office, he closed the door behind

me and dropped the blinds covering the windows, so no one from the war room could see inside.

"So, what brings you in today?" he asked, and I almost laughed at the absurdity of the question.

"I think we both know why I'm here." I tried to sound composed, but my damn voice cracked as I sat down across from him.

He looked older than the last time I'd seen him. His eyes bore more wrinkles around the edges, and the bags under them appeared bigger. Was he as worried as I was?

"You're going to have to be a little more specific, Dominic."

I decided to come right out with it. "I saw Dove this morning."

His eyes widened as he leaned back in his desk chair, the pressure making it squeak. "Did you talk to her?" The tone of his voice was almost animated.

Now, we were getting somewhere.

I nodded. "She'd asked me to meet her."

"What did she say?" he asked a little too quickly before he sucked in a loud, long breath. "Hell, Dominic, what did she ask you to do?"

Sometimes, Bob was too good at his job. He had the ability to put all the pieces in place before most people even realized that there was a puzzle to put together. Or maybe he just knew how Dove and I operated better than most.

"It doesn't matter what she said. What matters is, everything she didn't."

"I don't know what happened between the two of you," he said, and I had to stop myself from completely coming apart.

The idea that he, of all people, would simply accept that we broke up—*for any reason*—was beyond asinine.

"Nothing! That's just it, Bob. Nothing fucking happened! One minute, she was here, and the next, she was gone," I tried to explain, but I felt like nothing I was saying made any kind of sense. I still hadn't been able to figure out where we'd gotten so sideways, or why, or more importantly, how.

"That's not what she told me."

I blew out a sound of disgust. "I'm sure it isn't. But in what universe does us breaking up make sense to you? Tell me."

His lips pressed together in a straight line. He knew this was as fucked up as I did, but for whatever reason, he refused to admit it to me. Maybe it was his fatherly side that didn't allow him to see Dove as a deceiver, even when he knew that she was.

"There's only one thing I can think of." I looked him dead in the eyes. "She's doing this to either protect you or me. And I'm ninety-nine percent positive that there isn't anything worth a damn on me. I've been careful. So, I'm asking you, Bob … what could Trevor possibly have on you?"

Anyone else would have missed it. But I wasn't some nobody off the street. I knew this man inside and out. Knew that he wasn't perfect even though he always tried to be. So, I didn't miss the way his face started to turn ashen before he regained his composure. Or how his hands balled into fists so tight that his knuckles turned white before he put them in his lap, out of my view. Or the way his jaw clenched, forcing the muscles in the back of his mouth to flex with the pressure before he released it.

"No idea, son. I really don't."

"This isn't the time for games. She's going to marry

him! You have to tell me the truth. I can't lose her. I can't." I stumbled over the words he already had to know were true as what was left of my heart crashed to the floor at my feet.

"Dominic, pull yourself together. You're no good to me like this. Go home. I'll talk to Dove. And I'll be in touch."

Pull myself together? My fucking world was falling apart, and he wanted me to pull myself together?!

"Just tell me one thing," I said, and he waved a hand in the air, indicating that I should go ahead and ask. "You think this is messed up, right? Dove and Trevor? It doesn't add up to you, does it?"

He sat there, quiet for a beat too long, and I almost told him to forget it, but he finally spoke. "She insists that it's real. Her and Trevor. I know she's lying—I'm not stupid, son—but I don't know why. Before you came in here today, I figured she was protecting you. And since I heard hide nor hair from you since this *engagement*, I assumed you knew exactly why it was happening."

All this time, he'd thought this was somehow about me.

And he hadn't even considered trying to talk Dove out of it? Of course he hadn't. He would have known that if I was involved, there would be no reasoning with her.

"It's not me, Bob. And if it's not me, then …" I paused for dramatic effect, knowing that he could put two and two together without me having to spell it out for him.

"I'll be in touch," he said, and it sounded so cold.

I started thinking that he might be mad at me before realizing that his head had to be spinning, searching for whatever it could be that Trevor had on him if Dove wasn't protecting me.

"We have to save her," I breathed out.

He rose to his feet, stormed around the desk, and pulled me in for a hug.

A couple slaps to the back, and I pulled away, more emotional than I wanted to be when I left his office and walked into a room filled with watchful eyes and gossiping mouths, who would no doubt be focused on me. This entire town had been talking about me for months, but I'd done my best to block it out.

I wasn't sure how much longer I'd be able to pretend like what they said didn't matter.

DINNER WITH DAD

DOVE

I WASN'T IN the state of mind to play the dutiful and doting fiancée tonight, so I called Trevor and told him that I started my period unexpectedly. The kind that bled through tampons minutes after putting them in. I overly exaggerated, hoping to sufficiently gross him out enough that he'd keep his distance from me for at least a couple of nights. I needed to buy myself a little time.

"Dove, don't tell me things like that," he complained, his tone disgusted.

Even though he was pissed, he accepted my excuse. After, of course, he told me to take some Midol. Guys were so fucking clueless sometimes. Talk about a little blood and cramps, and they got all squeamish. Well, most guys anyway. Not Dominic … *of course*. He was always attentive and caring if I was ever in any kind of pain. It was like he couldn't bear to watch me hurting.

God, I miss him.

Picking up my cell, I stared at it for a second before double-checking all of my settings, like the kid at the phone store had shown me. He'd informed me that my location sharing had been turned on and that some of my apps had been set to share with Trevor only. I'd turned them all off and only allowed my location to be shared with two people—Dominic and my dad. I was pushing my luck whenever Trevor eventually found out, but this was one fight I wasn't giving in on. My being tracked twenty-four hours a day had not been part of the agreement.

I fired off a text to my dad, asking if he was home and if I could stop by. He always took too long to respond, and I should have just called him instead, but this time, his reply was instant.

> WAS GOING TO SEE WHAT YOU WERE UP TO TONIGHT, KIDDO. COME ON BY.

Responding that I'd be on my way soon, I changed quickly into more casual and comfortable clothes. I walked out to my Range Rover before wondering if it had a tracking device on it as well. I'd ask my dad to check for one once I got over there. I knew that he had some type of scanning tool that could tell us if there was anything on it.

My thoughts had been a tangled-up mess even more than usual. Seeing Dominic today had pushed me over the edge. I'd been able to pretend like keeping him at a distance was easy as long as there was no communication between us. But once I'd looked at him, all of those half-truths had been shot to hell.

When I pulled into the driveway, the garage door opened, and I saw my dad standing inside with a smile on his face. I smiled back, wishing he didn't look so old and tired. Cutting the engine, I stepped out, and he was right there, pulling me in for a hug.

"Is there any way to check if there's a tracking device on my car?" I asked, cutting right to the chase.

He pulled away from me, his eyes narrowing. "Do you think there might be?"

Nodding, I answered, "It's possible. I just want to be safe."

"Dove," he cautioned, "what's going on? Are you in

some sort of trouble?"

"*I'm* not." I emphasized the word *I'm*. "Can you check? It's just me being overly cautious and paranoid. Trevor's getting higher in the political circuit. It's not out of the question that his opponents might do something like that, right? Maybe bug my car to listen in?"

Once I started spinning the lie, the rest kept coming easily. It sounded plausible to me that Trevor's line of work might lead to some not-so-legal things happening to those he cared about. As his fiancée, I'd top that list.

"I guess not. I'll check. You go inside and make sure the food's not burning."

"You cooked?" I asked through my surprise, and he let out a deep laugh.

I walked through the garage door and into the house I'd grown up in. Two pizza boxes sat on top of the kitchen counter, and I shook my head. I knew he hadn't cooked! The man hadn't used anything other than the microwave since I'd moved out.

Opening up the cupboard, I pulled out two plates and set them on the table, where I'd moved the pizzas to as well. I was almost shocked the man still had any dishes left in the house. He was always eating off of paper plates or out of those horrible microwave meal containers.

My dad walked in and shook his head in my direction. "Car's all clean."

That was a relief, but not really unexpected. Pinging my phone had been the smarter move on Trevor's part. My phone was always with me, in my pocket or in my purse, and I didn't always take my car when I went places. Sometimes, I actually walked.

"Thank you for checking."

"Anytime, sweet pea," he said as he sat down at the table. "You pulled out the real plates, huh?"

"Yes. And you'll like it."

"You're washing them."

"Oh, washing two plates will be super challenging. Probably take me all night," I mocked.

"Don't sass me." He pointed a finger in my direction, but his mouth couldn't hide the grin that started forming.

I loved this man. Would do anything to protect him, and honestly, I wasn't even mad at him for putting me in this position. I could have been. Had every right to blame him for my predicament, but something inside me wouldn't allow it. It downright refused.

The scent of cheese and olive oil–baked crust hit my nose, and my stomach actually growled. I couldn't remember the last time I'd allowed myself to pig out on pizza. And it wasn't because I was trying to look svelte in my wedding dress. I couldn't care less what the hell I looked like on that day. It would be a miracle if my legs held me up at the altar if I wasn't standing next to Dominic. I wouldn't be surprised at all if they gave out and refused to work when it came right down to it. My mind could do its best to resist, but my body refused to betray him.

I'd barely had an appetite since breaking up with Dominic. I had to force myself to eat on a daily basis. Every bite was a struggle, each swallow threatening to give it all back before it even hit my empty stomach. Dominic had noticed the weight loss. I had seen him take every inch of me in with his eyes, the look on his face not happy.

"I had an unexpected visitor at the station today," my dad said, bringing my thoughts back to the present.

"Oh yeah? Who?" I asked.

"Dominic."

I had not been prepared for his answer even though I should have expected it, and I started choking. Had to reach for my glass of water and down the entire thing. How many times had I choked today? This was becoming an annoying trend.

"What did he want?" I tried to ask with as little emotion in my voice as possible, but it was a futile attempt at best.

"Well, he told me something interesting." He reached for a napkin and wiped at the corners of his mouth.

What could Dominic have said? I wondered as my body tensed. "What did he tell you?"

"You see, sweet pea, I always thought this whole *you and Trevor* thing was bullshit," he started, and I let out a gasp as he continued. "But I figured there was a reason you were going along with it. A reason I couldn't help with or talk you out of. Otherwise, you would have asked me."

He was getting too close. If my dad figured out why I was doing what I was, he wouldn't allow it. Bob Tryst always put me first even if it was to his detriment, and this would be no exception. I couldn't have him turning himself in and still be expected to live with myself after.

I started shaking my head vehemently. I needed him to stop asking questions. "No. It's not like that. Maybe you don't know Dominic as well as you think you do. Maybe he's not a good guy. Maybe he did something horrible to me and hurt me. Do you think I'd tell you if he had?"

Lies. Lies. Lies. They tasted so sour and vile in my mouth, and I wanted to spit them out and stomp all over them until they couldn't ever be spoken again.

"I can see that you're not ready to tell me the truth. But how am I supposed to stand by and watch you marry this guy when I know you don't want to?"

My dad had initially questioned it all when I first told him that I was engaged to Trevor. Granted, the dating, engagement, and wedding date all happened incredibly quickly. Trevor had said he had to rush it or else we'd be giving Dominic too much time to figure out a way to save me even though he hinted that doing so was impossible. Trevor was still worried. Dominic had always been too big of a threat to him.

Trevor had told everyone else, "When you know who

you are meant to be with, you don't see the sense in waiting to make them yours."

It was a slight at my and Dominic's courtship. From the outside, looking in, no one could understand why we weren't married already—or at least engaged. But neither one of us understood how a piece of paper was supposed to change anything between us. We weren't in a rush. We were committed and both focusing on growing our businesses. I wasn't ready to have kids yet.

Soon … but not quite yet.

If only we'd known what was headed straight for us, we would have rushed to the justice of the peace and made my marrying someone else not an option.

Again, my dad never believed any of it, even when I put on my best acting skills and brought Trevor home to formally meet him. I realized now that my dad had done me a kindness in letting it go at the time. I'd stupidly thought he'd bought what I was selling, but now, I knew that he never had.

"I do want to." I tried to sound resolved, but my voice shook. "I need to."

"Need isn't the same as want."

"Dad," I pleaded, "please let this go. If you don't, you'll only make it worse."

"How am I supposed to accept that? It's my job to keep you safe, Dove. I'm not doing my job."

"Listen to me," I implored, reaching across the table and taking his hand in mine.

His eyes looked even more tired now than they had when I first arrived, if that was even possible.

"I know what I'm doing, okay? Trust me that I'm figuring it out. But in the meantime, I need you to go along with it and not make any waves."

"At least tell me that Dominic has a plan," he said, sounding hopeful. Like if Dominic was involved somehow, then it would be easier for him to swallow what I was asking him to do.

I shook my head. "There can't be one. Especially not one involving him."

My dad leaned back in the chair and blew out a breath toward the ceiling. "I don't feel good about this."

"Do you trust me?" I asked. It was the only way to hopefully, maybe—*dear God, please*—get him to listen to me. "Dad. Do. You. Trust. Me?" I emphasized every word.

"Of course, I do."

"Then, you have to let me do this. Believe me, the second I can, I'll tell you everything."

"And in the meantime, what am I supposed to do?"

Pray that I figure a way out of this before the damn wedding day, was what I wanted to say, but I couldn't.

"Nothing."

OPERATION OBJECT

DOMINIC

I HATED BEING home … in our bedroom, lying in our bed. The pillowcases still smelled like Dove's shampoo. I couldn't tell you the number of times I'd pressed them to my face and inhaled, wishing she would be here when I opened my eyes. But she never was. And I was terrified that she might never be again. No matter how impossible the idea seemed to be, the truth was that she was slipping further and further away by the minute.

I should have called my father and asked him just what the hell was going on, and I'd debated doing it no less than a thousand times. Even showing up at the house and confronting him in person had crossed my mind, but there was no point to any of it. I knew he'd lie to me. As long as it benefited him—and this deal with Dove had to somehow—I'd never know the truth.

Thank God for my job. It was the only thing that even remotely kept my mind off of what I'd lost, what I was attempting to live without. Burying myself in work had proven to only be somewhat distracting. The problem was that I always ended up online, searching for articles on Trevor or my father, trying to figure out what exactly they were up to. I was never any closer than when I'd started.

My phone vibrated, and I reluctantly reached for it, knowing that it wouldn't be Dove on the other end so I struggled to care. I figured it might be Michael, asking me what the plan was. He was one hundred percent in on Operation Object—that was what we'd named it. At least it made me smile every time he mentioned it in a text.

I noticed Bob's name on the screen, and I pressed Answer as quickly as I could.

"Morning," I breathed into the line.

"Come over."

"Station or house?" I asked, knowing that just because it was the weekend, that didn't mean he wouldn't be at work.

"House," he said before ending the call.

It was abrupt and not at all like Bob, so I knew it had to be important. Throwing the covers off my body, I hopped out of bed like a madman and got dressed, trying to ignore the dresser drawers that were empty of Dove's things. They used to be so full that she could hardly close them. I'd promised to build her the closet of her dreams one day.

Just like I'd promised I'd propose.

And marry her.

And make her the mother of my children.

Now, that day was being threatened. Over my dead body.

I PARKED MY car on the curb in front of Bob's house and felt my chest tighten. This house had always been a second home to me, and now … now, I didn't know what it was. The front door opened before I reached it, and Bob stood on the other side, a serious expression on his face. He looked around, almost like he was checking if I'd been followed. Funny thing was, I'd done the same thing when I headed over here, glancing in the rearview mirror nonstop and taking an out-of-the-way route.

"I wasn't followed," I said, and he gave me a nod before throwing an arm around my shoulders and practically forcing me inside. "What's going on?"

"I saw Dove last night."

"Okay."

The house was still dark. He hadn't opened up any of the shades or curtains, and it almost made me forget that the sun was shining outside.

"Sit." He waved a hand toward the couch while he took a seat in his favorite worn-out recliner.

No matter how old I got, I'd always feel like a kid around Dove's dad.

"What'd she say? How'd she look? She's getting too thin."

He ran a hand down his face. "She ate pizza last night, so that was good."

I actually felt relieved, hearing that. It wasn't like my girl to not eat, but she looked like she hadn't been eating in who knew how long? Stress did that to a person.

"That is good."

"Yeah," he agreed before jumping into the rest. "She's

lying. About everything. But she won't tell me why. Trevor definitely has something on one of us." He wagged his finger between our two bodies. "You're sure it's not you?"

From applying for permits to getting loans and acquiring properties, I'd done it all legally and to the letter. A part of me had always known that if I skirted my way through any of the steps, it could be used against me somewhere down the line. People could always be turned against you, no matter who they were or how many times they insisted they wouldn't. Which was why I was never tempted to use my name, my father's stature, or ask for help along the way. What I'd created and done for the people in town was of my own accord and hard work.

Leaning forward, I put my elbows on my knees and looked him in the eyes. "I honestly can't think of anything. I've done everything by the books. Never asked for any favors. Never done anything illegal. I really don't think it's me. I don't see how it could be."

"Which leaves me, right? I mean, that's what you're thinking."

"That's my thought, yes. But what have you done? Is

there something?"

I wondered, if Bob Tryst had done something that would get him in serious trouble, would he even admit it to me? He was a proud man.

"I'm not sure."

That was as good of an answer as I was going to get. And in truth, it didn't matter anyway. It changed nothing. Dove was being coerced somehow, and I needed to stop it.

"I asked Dove last night if you had a plan, and she said that you couldn't have one."

That surprised me. "Really? Because when I saw her, she basically asked me to stop the wedding."

He leaned back into his chair and played with the corners of his mustache. I knew he was deep in thought in that moment and to not interrupt, so I waited. When he came back to the moment, his mouth was twisting up on one side.

"What did she tell you to do?"

"She asked me to object during the ceremony."

A loud laugh escaped his throat. "Ballsy. Wait, are you even invited?"

I blew out a quick huff and shrugged. "I have no idea,

but I don't think that was the point."

"Were you planning on doing this alone?"

"Michael said he'd help. I figured I'd need it."

He nodded in agreement. "That's good. That's real good. Trevor will be expecting you to do something, don't you think?"

I swallowed around the newly formed lump in my throat. Talking about this with Bob made it even more real. "I would assume so," I said, but I hadn't really considered that, if I was being honest.

I counted on Michael helping to distract people, if necessary, but now, I wasn't so sure what else I might need him to do. He and I needed a better plan. I'd make sure to call him as soon as I left here to have him meet me at my house, so we could go over all the possibilities.

"Do you have the wedding details?" Bob pushed up from his chair and started walking toward the kitchen before disappearing behind a wall, still within hearing range.

"Next Saturday. I figured the rest would be easy to find out." I could have asked a hundred people for the information and gotten it easily. I just hadn't done it yet.

"Here." He returned and handed me a thick card.

It had Dove's and Trevor's names on it in some kind of horrible writing you could barely make out along with the date, time, and location of the ceremony, followed by reception information.

Grabbing my cell, I snapped a picture of only the details and tried to hand the invitation back to Bob, but he waved me off.

"You keep it," he said, and my throat tightened.

"I'd rather not." I dropped it on the coffee table and averted my eyes. I never wanted to see that fucking piece of paper again.

"Okay. So, your plan is to get into the ceremony and object when the time is right?" he asked before frowning. "Does objecting actually stop anything? I've never been to a wedding where someone did that before."

I had no idea. All I knew was that Dove had asked me to do it, and so it was what I was going to do. The rest of the details hadn't mattered to me.

"I don't know. I guess we're going to find out."

"I'll second you. When you object, I'll agree to it," he said.

I suddenly felt sick to my stomach. If Trevor or my father had information on Bob, him objecting could make it all come out. And whatever it was had to be bad enough that Dove was actually going through with this charade.

"I don't need you to do that." I tried to sway him from the idea.

"You can't stop me," he challenged, and I knew he was right.

What was I going to do, put a gag over his mouth when I stepped inside?

"Fine. Play it by ear. When the time comes, if it feels right to second me, do it. But no hard feelings if you don't."

"Fine," he agreed, but his tone was a little snarky, and I knew it was time for me to leave.

There was nothing more to say. The two of us were at our wits' end, both feeling helpless with no one to blame but ourselves.

"I guess I'll see you and Michael next Saturday then."

I nodded before turning to go. "See you next Saturday."

"Dominic," Bob said, and I stopped walking, but didn't

turn around to face him. “Don’t mess this up.”

I didn’t say anything in response. I simply continued walking out of his front door and toward my car, sensing that he was watching my every move.

Messing up wasn’t an option. I had to get Dove back.

I DO … *N'T*

DOVE

I STARED AT my reflection in the giant mirror, feeling the exact opposite of how I always assumed I'd feel on my wedding day. There was no joy reflected back at me, no hope in my eyes, no blissful happiness etched into my smile lines.

There was only dread.

This was it. The day part of my life ended and everything I'd ever dreamed of being—mostly Mrs. DeLuca—slipped out of my grasp. Whenever I stopped the wheels from spinning and comprehended what I was about to do and exactly who would be waiting for me at the end of that long aisle, my heart started racing, my chest tightened, and I struggled to take in air.

My vision blurred.

I was in a full-on panic. *How can I get out of this? What the hell am I doing?*

My dad, my dad, my dad, I chanted as I willed myself to calm down.

After I inhaled deep breaths before blowing them out slowly, my heart attempted to return to a normal speed. My body, which had started to break out into a cold sweat, stopped.

I closed my eyes tight and got a handle on my thoughts and emotions. If there was one thing I was good at doing, it was compartmentalizing. I could close things out of my mind and pretend they weren't happening with the best of them. Dominic always called it my superpower. I called it denial. Regardless of which one it was, it worked. And right now, I needed it to work more than ever.

There was a quick knock on the door before it creaked opened slightly as my dad's voice asked, "Can I come in?"

"Of course," I answered, my body already ten times calmer than it had been a moment before.

I can do this. I have to do this.

"Hey, sweet pea." He entered the room, his eyes sweeping across the small space before landing on me with a mixture of awe and sadness in his expression.

He was going to make me lose it and ruin my makeup if he didn't stop looking at me like that.

"You look so handsome, Dad," I gushed.

I'd never seen him in a tuxedo before. Before I could compliment him more, I reminded myself that we were only here because I was being blackmailed, and instead of going soft inside, I hardened.

"Thank you." He stepped toward me and reached for my hand, taking it in his. "I know this isn't real, but, gosh, you look so beautiful. You look just like your mom."

"Dad," I warned, needing him to stop. "Don't make me cry. Not today. Not for this." It was the admittance I hadn't given him before even though he had always sensed the truth.

I sucked in another steadying breath, and my resolve cemented. Tears weren't acceptable. This wasn't a joyous occasion, and we both knew it. I'd be faking it the rest of the day for hundreds of people; I refused to pretend when it was just the two of us.

"You don't have to do this. Whoever you're protecting, it's not worth it. Even if you're protecting me,

Dove." He reached for my shoulders and held me tight, forcing me to look him in the eyes. "We can leave right now."

"I know, Dad."

It was such a sweet offer, and I knew he meant it, but I could never do that to him.

"So, you want to get out of here?" He thumbed toward the door with a grin.

"I can't."

It wasn't the answer he wanted to hear, but he'd expected it nonetheless. I could tell. His shoulders deflated before he stiffened back up. Maybe I'd gotten my resolve from him.

"I need to finish getting ready. Don't forget to come back and get me."

"Never." He planted a soft kiss on my cheek before leaving me alone once again.

My thoughts drifted to Dominic, like they usually did. I'd never reached out and told him not to come today. Part of me knew that he wouldn't have believed me if I'd said I hadn't meant what I asked him to do. He'd definitely think it was some kind of game then, but he wouldn't know which part I was playing. So, I had decided to say nothing and see what happened.

Plus, I wanted him to show up, proverbial guns blazing. Of course I wanted that. Dominic simply standing idly by while I *married* some other man made me want to break everything in this room. He'd never let that happen. This was my knight in shining armor we were talking about. My ride or die. My partner in crime. My other half. My *soul mate*. We did not exist apart. It didn't work that way.

So, of course he would come. Of course he would do what I'd asked. Any other option was unfathomable.

And then I'd have to deal with the consequences.

A shadow crossed in front of one of the windows, drawing my attention toward it, and for a split second, I thought he was here. But when I stood up to look, there was nothing but tree branches and overgrown bushes.

A knock at the door distracted me, and I turned away from the glass.

"Dove, it's me," Kristina said.

"Come in."

She blew into the room like she floated on air. "Dove,

you look stunning."

I wanted to laugh. The dress I was wearing was absolutely ridiculous. An enormous A-line ball gown that couldn't have been less my style. It hid every curve I had, and the bottom was so puffy that I could fit at least three small children under there. It was a dress that didn't suit my style at all, but if this wedding was a sham, then my dress would be too. The least I could do was look the opposite of myself in every way even if I was the only one who knew it. I planned on saving my dream dress for the real thing, fuck you very much.

"Don't say that," I mumbled under my breath before catching myself.

Even though I'd given her a one-worded answer that told her everything she'd suspected not that long ago, I hadn't confessed the whole truth to her, and I never planned to. No matter how many times she asked. The last thing I needed was to involve anyone else in this scheme and potentially get them hurt as well. Enough people were hurt already and I was afraid Trevor had no limits when it came to this.

"What?"

"I said, thank you," I lied.

"No, you didn't," she said, calling me out, but not pushing. "You really do look gorgeous."

I didn't care how I looked.

"Is he here?" I asked, and she knew who I was referring to without my having to call him by name.

"I haven't seen him. Figured if he was, there would be all kinds of commotion."

I couldn't disagree with that assessment.

Trevor had initially wanted Dominic to come today. Reveled in the very idea actually. Said that he wanted to witness Dominic lose everything he'd ever loved in real time. He thrived off the notion that Dominic would be devastated to the point of no return. The thought alone decimated me.

But somewhere along the way, Trevor changed his mind. He deemed Dominic too disruptive, potentially dangerous, and a time bomb waiting to explode, even with the threat I carried on my shoulders. Trevor knew that Dominic wasn't aware of the blackmail, so he couldn't be trusted to stay calm and collected … not when I was involved. Dominic's father had tried to insist that he be allowed to attend, claiming it would be good for the town to see a strong man fall to his knees, but Trevor stood firm in his new decision. He'd refused to allow it.

Not like lack of an invitation could stop Dominic anyway.

"Are you sure you're ready to do this?" Kristina asked. She was being sweet, thinking she was giving me a way out.

"Ready as I'll ever be."

That was at least the truth.

"I'll go get your dad. It's almost time."

"Thank you."

"I'll see you out there."

She closed the door behind her. I wasn't having anyone stand up at the altar with me. Trevor and I would be alone while we lied to an entire room filled with friends, family, and mostly strangers. At least, they were to me. I hadn't been around Trevor long enough to meet all of the people within his political circles who would be in attendance, and I only knew a couple of his big donors.

"Sweet pea, I'm coming in." My dad appeared, adjusted his tie, and reached for my hand before placing it around his arm. “We can still bail,” he suggested one last time, but I gripped him a little tighter, letting him know that I wasn't leaving.

“Is he here?”

“Haven't seen him,” he said, his voice sounding almost as disappointed as I felt.

Where the hell is Dominic? It was getting late.

The double doors swung open at the same time as the processional music filled the air. I must have blacked out on the walk down the aisle or gone into some kind of trance because the next thing I knew, I was standing in front of the altar in a massive church, staring at Trevor O'Connor's demonic blue eyes, and I had absolutely no idea how the hell I'd gotten there.

The smile he wore took up his whole face, and I wondered if I was the only one who saw how fake it was, how downright cruel and malicious. He wasn't smiling because he was happy or overjoyed to see me standing there with him.

He was grinning because he thought he'd won.

And as I looked out into the crowd, frantically searching for any sign of Dominic there, I thought that he might be right.

The minister started talking, saying things I didn't pay any attention to. My mind was elsewhere, my anger rising. *He really didn't come?* I couldn't fathom it. Refused to believe it.

As if on cue, the minister announced, "If there is anyone here who sees any reason why these two shall not be committed in holy matrimony, speak now or forever hold your peace."

My eyes flew to my dad, who looked half-tempted to stand up. I gave him a quick shake of my head, hoping he'd listen, before I frantically searched the rest of the church for the dark eyes that I'd know anywhere, but Dominic wasn't here. I held my breath and waited for him to speak up from wherever he was hiding, but there was only silence.

He hadn't come for me.

He didn't care anymore.

We truly were over.

"I object! These two should not be married!"

The boastful voice of the person I'd never expected to say those words struck my ears with such force that I had to pinch myself to make sure I wasn't dreaming. I felt my shoulders sag with relief… and amazement. Trevor looked horrified.

Was this some sort of trick?

SAVE MY WOMAN

DOMINIC

OPERATION OBJECT WAS in full effect. Michael and I drove to the church where the wedding was taking place, and I parked a few blocks away, so I wouldn't draw any attention to the fact that I was there. An anonymous email had informed me that I wasn't invited and then warned me not to show up. It only fueled me to do the opposite. Trevor had to have known that it would.

Michael and I had scouted this location the other day, noting how many entrances and windows there were around the building. I'd even drawn a really crappy map, and now, I could barely even read my chicken scratch.

"You go left. I'll take right. Meet up at the tree," I directed, and Michael gave me a thumbs-up before taking off.

Holding the crude drawing in my hand, I walked around my side of the building, checking each doorway and tugging on windows. Each one I checked was locked firmly in place. I'd actually expected that to be the case, considering that it had been renovated with air-conditioning about twenty years back. Before the addition, the windows were always opened at least halfway to let the fresh air in.

What I hadn't considered was the fact that Dove would be viewable behind one of those locked windows. Hadn't emotionally prepared for what seeing her would do to me. Dressed for a wedding, but not marrying me. Her oversize white ball gown caught my eye. It wasn't even remotely her taste, but she still looked absolutely stunning in it. She was so damn beautiful that it caused me physical pain to look at her. I watched for only a few seconds, stopping myself from tapping on the glass to get her attention. If her green eyes had turned and met mine, I would have lost it completely. Nothing could have stopped me from shattering the window and dragging her out of it.

What was left of my heart started pounding so hard in my chest that I was convinced she could hear it. I bolted, finished my check, and headed across the street to meet Michael. He was already waiting for me under a giant shaded tree. We were far enough away that no one would see us unless they were specifically looking, but close enough that we had a bird's-eye view of who was coming and going. There were so many people I didn't recognize.

"Well?" Michael asked, raising his eyebrows in question. "Mine were all locked. What about yours?"

"Locked. Only doors accessible are the main ones. And they're guarded." I gave a nod toward the men stationed out front, greeting the guests and checking their invitations before allowing them access inside.

"Didn't really expect security. Did you?" Michael asked, his voice a mixture of nerves and excitement.

I actually hadn't counted on that. It never crossed my mind that Trevor would go that far to either keep me out or keep Dove in.

"Bit over the top, don't you think?" I played it off like it was no big deal, but six against two wasn't going to be easy.

Michael narrowed his eyes as he stared across the street, his hand shielding his gaze. "I don't recognize any of them."

I double-checked his assessment. "Me neither."

It was unfortunate that we didn't know any of the men. It would have made things at least a little easier.

"Okay. So, there're six of them and two of us."

My brain spun. I had no idea what to do that didn't involve trying to fight our way inside. Fighting would be loud, and the last thing I wanted was to make a huge scene prior to even getting in the chapel.

"Maybe once the ceremony starts, they'll change their positions? Go inside or guard Trevor at the altar?" I said my thoughts out loud.

"No. Zero chance the doors are left unguarded during any part of the ceremony," Michael said matter-of-factly, like he was some sort of all-knowing super spy.

He was right though. Trevor clearly wasn't messing around, and he wouldn't be that stupid. The only way in or out wouldn't be left unattended.

"All right. Then, we have two options." I started to explain, and Michael was all ears, listening intently. "We either hope they don't know who we are and try to talk our way in or—"

"Or?" he interrupted quickly.

"We fight."

Michael got a shit-eating grin on his face. The guy loved a good fight, but I loved a fair one. Six against two wasn't necessarily the best odds. At least, not in our favor.

"We can do both if it comes down to it," I said because we were running out of time.

Guests seemed to be trickling in now instead of in larger clusters. The guards were continually glancing over their shoulders and looking around instead of eyeballing each incoming person.

Michael waved his fingers in the air like he was calling me toward him. "Hit me," he said, and I knew he was waiting for me to tell him my plan, not actually strike him.

"We try to go inside like we were invited. Guests of the wedding. If that doesn't work, we fight. They won't be expecting us to get physical."

"I'll hit first," he suggested. "That way, they'll be focused on me, and you can run in while they're scrambling."

I actually felt hopeful for the first time all day. Surely, at least one of us would be able to get inside if the other one was subdued.

"Okay, it's now or never."

"Let's roll."

Straightening my jacket and adjusting my tie, I walked across the street as cool and as calm as my body allowed. Inside, I was a wreck. This had to work.

The two of us were closing in on the stairs when all six of the guards suddenly took position, blocking the only entrance.

"Excuse me," I said, and they stared me down, refusing to move.

"Can I see your invitations?" a big, tough guy asked.

"We're men. We don't keep those things." Michael tried to sound reasonable, but Big, Tough Guy wasn't having it.

"You're not welcome, Mr. DeLuca. You either," Big, Tough Guy said as he puffed out his chest.

He wasn't taller than me, but he looked like he'd eaten someone my size for breakfast that morning.

"I was invited," I spat, straightening my shoulders and standing tall.

Technically, I hadn't been, but who cared at this point?

I needed to get inside.

"Mr. O'Connor gave specific instructions that you were not to be allowed in. And we were told to keep you out by any means necessary." He actually grinned as he said the last sentence and tossed a look over his shoulder to the rest of his crew.

I'd wondered what the guards were truly here for, and now, I had my answer. They weren't here to protect Trevor or keep him safe from threats or harm. They were here for me. To stop me. Trevor had known I'd never be able to stay away, so he'd thought of everything.

There was no way in hell I was letting him win. Not when my woman was involved. I pretended to accept my defeat and turned to walk away before clenching my fists and giving Michael a quick nod. He yelled out with joy before socking one of the guards right in the rib cage, catching him unaware and causing him to lose his breath as he bent over in pain.

I threw my right hand as hard as I could into Big, Tough Guy's nose and watched as blood started pouring out. He reached for his face, wiping the blood away like it was nothing but a minor nuisance. Someone grabbed me from behind, and I struggled to move my upper body. Whoever it was had my arms in a vise grip.

Big, Tough Guy was suddenly in front of me, his hand gripping my throat. I fought to take in air, my eyes rolling back into my head as I grew dizzy.

And day turned into night.

I FAILED HER

DOMINIC

MY EYES SLOWLY opened as I struggled to focus on my surroundings. Everything was a blurry mess. The ground felt cold as I pressed my hand against it and moved it around, my fingers pressing into the dips and texture. Tile. I was on a tiled floor. Looking up, I recognized the hazy doorway. I was in my house.

What the hell happened? I struggled to remember anything.

Pushing my body up into a sitting position, I scooted back until I hit the wall and relaxed against it. I glanced around once my vision returned. Michael was a short distance away, still passed out. At least, I hoped he was only asleep and not actually dead.

I didn't have the energy to check; my body wasn't

ready to move willingly. And thankfully, I didn't have to because he started moaning soon after.

"Are we in your house?" he mumbled.

"Apparently," I said, but talking hurt. Moving hurt. Everything fucking hurt.

"How'd we get here?" he asked as I grabbed my aching head.

"I have no idea," I responded, but my voice was scratchy.

"Were we drugged?" Michael asked.

The thought had crossed my mind. This wasn't just getting knocked out cold by a sucker punch. My head spun like something foreign had entered my body and it was fighting to get it out.

"It's possible." I fingered the sides of my neck, feeling for any kind of puncture wound.

Dove and I had been obsessed with the show *Dexter* when it first came out, and we'd watched every episode twice. Knocking someone out with a ketamine-filled needle to the neck seemed easy enough, and no one ever saw it coming.

My neck felt sore to the touch, but I wasn't sure if it

was my imagination or not. I needed a mirror. Or the camera on my cell. Desperately searching for my phone, I breathed out in relief when I found it still in my pocket, where I'd put it earlier. I pulled it out and opened the Camera app. Turning my head to the side, I snapped a picture before enlarging it.

I noticed multiple markings that hadn't been there before, but I assumed those were from the fight. I'd clearly been choked. My neck was bruised, and what looked like finger marks dotted the sides underneath my jaw.

"Maybe we really were drugged. After being choked unconscious," I said out loud.

Would Trevor have really gone to such lengths to ensure that I wouldn't screw things up? It seemed extreme. And not to mention, a little psychotic.

Blowing out a quick breath, I tried to stand up. My legs didn't want to cooperate, and I slammed my palms against the wall to stop myself from falling. This was ridiculous. My stomach recoiled from the movements, and I vomited all over the floor.

"Fuck," I said after wiping my mouth with my hand and reaching for the handle on the front door.

"Where are you going?" Michael asked, his body still in the fetal position, facing me.

"I want to see if my car's here or not."

The door opened, and I braced for sunlight, but I was met with the setting sun. *How long have we been out?* My car was sitting in the driveway, perfectly parked. So, not only had we been rendered unconscious and taken from the church, but we'd also been driven *in my car* and dropped off *inside my home*. Looking down, I spotted the keys sitting on the floor. Thank God I hadn't thrown up on them.

"Is it there?"

"Yeah."

"Is my truck still here?"

"Right where you left it," I said after noticing it was still parked at the curb. It looked untouched.

"They know what kind of car you drive and where you live. Think they'll be back?"

"Nah," I said. I honestly wasn't worried about that. There was nothing here that they needed, or they would have already taken it while we were knocked out. "I'm sure Trevor gave them detailed instructions. Especially if we were the whole reason those guys were at the church in the first place."

It seemed logical. If Trevor's intention was to keep me out, then the guards had literally one job. And that job was completed. No matter how much it pissed me off.

"Makes sense, I guess," Michael groaned and rolled over. "He didn't want you to stop the wedding, so he made sure you couldn't."

"It's crazy though, right?" I asked as I struggled to walk in his direction.

Michael was closer to the living room, and all I wanted to do was lie down on the couch.

"Of course it's crazy. But it's Trevor, so nothing surprises me. Absolutely nothing. Not when it comes to you. The guy hates you, Dom. He's insanely jealous, and he always has been."

I would never understand that. I'd never competed with Trevor for anything. If something meant that much to him, I always backed off. Dove was the only thing I hadn't been willing to give up. And now, he had her. As his *wife*.

My stomach threatened to lose it again, but I quickly lay down and brought my knees forward to try to calm it.

"Think Dove will ever forgive you?" Michael asked, and I wanted to fucking die.

He knew her as well as I did in certain ways. Like the fact that she could hold a grudge until the end of time and wasn't quick to forgive when she felt slighted.

"Probably not," I answered, like it even mattered. Nothing mattered anymore. "Are you ever going to get up?" I chastised my friend, knowing that he had to feel as shitty as I did.

His pain gave me the slightest sense of joy. See, I needed someone to feel as badly as I did. It made me feel less alone.

"I saw what happened to you when you got up. I'm not ever moving again."

"Me neither. I live here now. On this couch. Forward my mail," I said before closing my eyes as my head spun.

The next time I opened them, Michael was gone, and my phone was blacked out on the coffee table in front of me. I had no idea how long I'd been asleep for, no recollection of what day it was or the time. Fumbling around for a charger, I pulled the cord from underneath the couch and plugged my phone in.

Waiting the few minutes for it to fire up was torture, so I got up, grabbed the bottle of water that someone—assuming Michael—had left for me, and downed the whole thing in one gulp. I was definitely dehydrated. Heading toward the front door, where I'd tossed my cookies, I noticed that it was spotless. Michael was a damn good friend.

Filling up the bottle, I drank half of it before my stomach warned me to take it easy. I sat back down on the couch and grabbed my phone, turning it on. It buzzed in my hand, the date and time flashing, before it started ringing out notification after notification. My head spun as I did the math. I'd slept for over twenty-four hours straight, and I still felt like shit.

Missed calls, voice mails, and text messages beeped out. Unless they were from Dove, I couldn't care less about any of them.

No one else mattered.

Scanning the alerts, I finally saw her name in a text bubble. I pressed on my Messages app, and her name taunted me from the very top of the list. Usually, that would mean that she was the last person to reach out, but I had her contact pinned to the top, so she was always in that position.

I opened it as fast as I could, and my eyes scanned the date first.

Yesterday.

She'd sent this message yesterday morning, and I was only seeing it now. My jaw ticced as I read her words.

I HATE YOU.

AND I'LL NEVER FORGIVE YOU.

Of course she hated me. She was someone else's wife now, and I'd never forgive myself for letting that happen.

DEPRESSED AND ALONE

DOVE

I OSCILLATED BETWEEN being so unbelievably sad to downright angry. My emotions swirled and mixed inside my head until it ached. My heart refused to believe that Dominic had abandoned me when I needed him most.

But it was the truth, and I had to keep reminding myself of it.

He hadn't shown up. And I hadn't heard from him since.

He'd read my text message. A full day after I'd sent it, I saw that it had finally been opened. I'd thought waiting for that notification had been torture, but not getting a response from him was even worse. I spent all day wondering what he was thinking and doing and questioning how he could stay away from me like I never mattered to him at all. It wasn't like Dominic to be so reasonable when it came to me … to us.

I was sure he could be asking himself the same thing in regard to me, but I wasn't the one who hadn't followed through. I wasn't the one who hadn't shown up after asking me to and left him hanging ever since. We always fought for each other—*always*.

He should have been blowing up my phone nonstop, begging for my forgiveness, or at least trying to explain why he'd failed to show. But he hadn't done a single thing. People always said that *no response is a response*, so I guessed I had some sort of answer even though it wasn't even remotely the one I wanted and it didn't make any kind of sense. Him walking away without saying a word wasn't like him at all. It wasn't our MO. It wasn't what we did.

Something must have changed.

And I'd never ever forgive him for it.

IT HAD ONLY been a handful of days since the wedding, and I spent the majority of my time at my real estate office. I hated being at home. Plus, it was easier to distract myself and keep busy if I was surrounded by paperwork and incoming queries that needed answering. There was always a lot going on when it came to buying, selling, or renting properties. Hopetown seemed to be in a constant state of growth, which was a good thing in regard to my business but sort of sad when I got all sentimental about it, wishing it would never change.

My cell phone rang, and I glanced at it, no longer hoping to see Dominic's name on the other end. Okay, that was a lie. I wasn't sure I'd ever not hope to see his name flashing across my screen. Each day that passed without a word from him made me question everything I'd ever believed about us.

How was he not dying inside? Was he moving on without me?

My phone rang again, and I looked down and saw his father's name on the screen.

I swallowed my distaste before deciding to answer it. I owed it to him for what he'd done for me.

"Hello?" I said, sounding bored.

"Dove," he breathed out my name. "I need you to get

ahold of Dom and bring him to me right away."

My lips instantly snarled. Even though I was pissed off at Dominic and refused to forgive him, I'd still never betray him. Especially when it came to his father.

"Why would I do that?"

"Because if you don't, he might not live to see his next birthday."

"What the hell is wrong with you?" I snapped into the line. Who said things like that about their own kid?

"I *need* you to do this for me, Dove," he said with a little desperation and not at all like the overly confident man I'd always known.

If I was interpreting his tone correctly, he even sounded slightly fearful. I'd never heard him that way before. It was a bit unnerving.

"He won't take any calls from me. But he'll pick up if you call him. It's the least you can do, don't you think?"

I almost laughed out loud into the line, but I refused to give him the satisfaction of hearing it. The man had always claimed to love my laugh. Of course he'd throw what he'd done for me in my face. He probably would hold it over me for the rest of my life.

"Fine. What do you need me to do?"

He gave me some quick and easy instructions, and I sucked in a deep breath before hanging up, annoyed that he was using me to get to Dominic and confused about the threat.

Stepping out of my office, I must have had a concerned look on my face because Kristina stopped me in my tracks, her body blocking mine from leaving.

"Are you okay?"

"Yeah. I'll be right back. I have to go do something for Dominic's father."

She pursed her lips and shook her head. "Do you want me to come with you?"

"No, it's fine. I'll be quick," I said reassuringly.

The last thing I needed was for Kristina to worry more about me. The girl had been worked up for months, hating that she couldn't save me or at least help in some way.

"Call me if that changes," she said seriously, and I gave her a half-smile.

Her offer was sweet but pointless. I'd never involve anyone else in this sort of thing.

I exited the office and clicked the remote on my car. It

beeped, and the driver's door only let out a solo click. I'd adjusted the settings to stop unlocking the entire car at once in case someone tried to jump in on the passenger side while I wasn't paying attention. Ever since the wedding, I'd been overly paranoid that I was being watched or followed, that my life was in danger—or worse, my dad's. I glanced around quickly, checking my surroundings before hopping in.

I decided to call Dominic from the car while I headed toward the designated spot. There was no way I was letting him go into a meeting with his father alone. Whatever Mr. DeLuca had to say to Dominic, he would say it in front of me as well. I was sure he'd already planned on that.

Dominic didn't confront the people in our lives alone. We were a team.

Or at least, we used to be. My heart ached with the thought.

I was about to instruct my phone to dial Dominic when I spotted him getting out of his parked car. My insides burned with rage as I neared him. Pressing down on the gas, I thought for a second about running him over. That would teach him to abandon me. My car squealed to a stop instead. Dominic whirled around, his dark eyes wide with surprise and shock and then murder once he realized it was me behind the wheel.

Dove. I watched him mouth my name before he stormed over to the driver's side of my car.

I rolled down the window, not caring that people were watching our interaction. I didn't care about anything anymore. "I hate you." The words tumbled out of my mouth as my heart laughed. Hatred was the furthest thing in the world I could ever feel for this man.

"Get out of the car," he growled, and I narrowed my eyes, wishing they'd spear him with darts or something equally as painful. "Park the car and get out. Now."

He knew exactly what he was doing to me, and no matter how strong I wanted to be in his presence, I relented because he had demanded it of me. This man knew how to push my buttons and make me want to drop my panties and sit on his lap, all while yelling at him.

When I parked in the space next to his, shut the car off, and stepped out, Dominic was instantly at my side, towering over me, his shoulders large, his presence looming, my back pressed against the door. I had nowhere else to go. I couldn't move. He grabbed my arm and pulled me toward a building and then around the side, where no one could see or hear us. He made sure we weren't followed before he fell apart in front of me.

"Why the hell are you so mad at me? I'm mad at you, Dove. I'm fucking broken, baby. So fucking broken. I don't know how to breathe without you."

That admission killed me. I hadn't expected it. I couldn't hold it together anymore. Every emotion from the past few months came pouring out, and I completely lost it, tears spilling down my face. Dominic pulled me against him and held me tight, his chest moving in and out with his ragged breaths. It felt like years since I'd been in his arms. I would have been okay with dying right then and there.

"How could you do this to us, baby?" he asked, his breath hot against my head as he held me tight.

Does he not know? Is it possible that he doesn't know?

He moved away and looked down at me, his lips so close to mine that I couldn't think about anything other than having them. They were my lips. Pressing up on my tiptoes, I moved toward him slowly, giving him a chance to deny me even though I knew he never would. Or hoped he wouldn't. I wasn't so sure anymore.

His mouth was all over mine in an instant, claiming, nipping, owning. "Tell me you belong to me, baby. Tell me you're mine," he said desperately between kisses, and the feel of his tongue almost made my knees give out entirely.

This was where I belonged.

"Always and only yours." It had been too long since I'd felt him, and I never wanted it to stop.

But Dominic came to his senses, or something had triggered him because he pulled away abruptly, leaving me kissing nothing but the air.

"No," he said, wiping at his mouth. "Dammit."

"What's the matter? Dominic, what's wrong?"

"What's wrong? What's wrong?" he asked in a shout before pulling at his dark strands. I'd never seen him so worked up before. "I need to know everything that happened right fucking now, Dove," he said, and my entire body started shaking.

It was time to tell him the truth.

"Okay," I said softly, the tears still rolling down my

cheeks.

"Okay?" he repeated, like he couldn't believe I was being so agreeable.

"Yes. Of course I'll tell you anything you want to know."

He started pacing back and forth in quick movements, like I'd caught him off guard, and now, he wasn't sure where to start or what to ask exactly.

"Okay"—he stopped moving and faced me—"why did you say yes to Trevor?"

Easy. "He threatened my dad." I was as matter-of-fact as I could be.

"I knew it," he blew out. "I fucking knew it. What does he have on your dad?"

"He threatened to turn him in. Said he had information on my dad accepting bribes. He wanted to send my dad to prison." I stared at the ground instead of at him. I hated telling him this. I didn't want Dominic to look at my dad differently or think less of him.

He shook his head like he refused to believe it. "I don't think so, Dove. Your dad and I talked. Multiple times. Did Trevor show you any proof?"

I swallowed hard. "He showed me grainy video, but he mentioned a name. It was the same guy who had come to the house in high school. Remember that night?" I asked even though I already knew the answer.

"I remember."

My phone dinged out a notification from my purse, and I snapped out of the momentary reunion we were having and remembered what I was here for in the first place.

"Your father, Dominic," I started to say. "He needs to see you."

"Who cares?"

Typical Dominic.

"I know. Normally, I wouldn't either, but he called me."

"He called you? What did he want?" He sounded angry as he took a step toward me.

Dominic didn't like his family being in touch with me, like I was their friend or pawn when I was neither.

"He said that he needed to see you. Insinuated that you would be in some kind of danger if he didn't get to talk to you. That's why I'm here."

Dominic looked unhinged. Like he was going to turn around and punch the brick wall if he knew I wouldn't try to stop him. "In danger? What the hell does that mean? That's ridiculous. It's a ploy."

I didn't think this was funny or something to joke about, but then again, he hadn't heard the fear in his father's voice. Reaching out, I cupped his cheek with my hand, so he'd focus on me. His wild eyes met mine and held.

"Your father didn't sound like himself on the phone at all. He sounded worried. He needed me to reach out to you to make this meeting happen. Knew you wouldn't come otherwise."

He pulled his face from my touch, and I tried not to show my disappointment. "So, that's why you're here? Because my father sent you?"

He was testing me. Pushing me. Desperate to hear that I still loved him and wasn't doing this for anyone else but myself.

"I'd do anything to keep you safe."

"That's my job," he said instantly, all of his defenses dropping. He looked so tired.

"You sound like my dad." I wanted to smile but couldn't.

"Wait. Did my father say he'd hurt me?" Dominic sounded so betrayed.

The two of them might not have had the greatest relationship, but thinking that your own flesh and blood would stoop that low had to be devastating on some level.

"No, he didn't." I tried to keep him calm. "It sounded like someone else might hurt you and that he wouldn't be able to stop them."

Dominic shook his head before he started rubbing at his eyes. "This isn't right. My father might be a liar and a con artist, but—"

"I know," I interrupted his train of thought. "I think he might be in deep with some bad people."

"What do you mean?"

My brain had already run through a few different scenarios since I'd hung up the phone with his father. I couldn't help it or stop the wheels from spinning if I tried. "I think he's using his influence to protect someone. I think that's who is threatening you. It has to all be tied together somehow."

Dominic's father stepped out of the shadows from the back of the building, and we both froze in place. I had no idea how long he'd been there, listening to us.

"Smart girl, Dove."

PUTTING THE PIECES TOGETHER

DOMINIC

MY BODY INSTINCTIVELY moved in front of Dove's. I pushed her behind me in a protective stance, shielding her from my father. If he wanted to get anywhere near her, he'd have to go through me.

"Father."

"Son," he said.

I outwardly winced and watched as he closed the space between us in long strides, looking around to make sure we were still hidden from other prying eyes. We were. I'd already made sure of it earlier. But I guessed I'd forgotten to check behind the building, assuming that no one loitered around back there.

"You know, I really thought you'd show up at the

church and stop the wedding. I'd counted on it actually," he said out of nowhere, and I hoped I looked as shocked as I felt.

I'd always assumed that he set the whole *Dove marrying Trevor* thing up, so me stopping the wedding wouldn't have been in his best interest. If that were true, then what was he talking about?

"You counted on it? You counted on me showing up and stopping the wedding?" I repeated everything he'd just said.

"Yes. I never thought you'd let Dove marry anyone else. Especially not Trevor."

"Then, you should have at least left a window open or unlocked a door," I said, my irritation seeping into my tone.

Dove sucked in an audible breath that sounded too much like a sob.

I turned around to face her. "What is it, baby?"

"You were there that day?"

"Of course I was there. You didn't know?" I touched her face softly, and she leaned into it as her green eyes pierced right through me.

"No, I didn't know. I thought you never showed up. I figured I'd asked too much of you. That I'd finally pushed you too far. And so, you didn't come. I assumed you were done with me."

I wanted to throw her over my shoulder and never let her out of my grasp again. "I couldn't get in. All the windows and doors were locked. Trevor had six security guards stationed at the main entrance. They were expecting me. They knew I'd show up, and they were under strict instruction to use whatever force necessary to stop me from gaining entry. Six on two is never a fair fight, baby, but I promise you that I tried."

"Two? Who else was with you?" my father inquired, drawing my focus back toward him.

"Michael. Pretty sure we were drugged."

"I guess Trevor's *not* as stupid as he looks," my father said smugly.

"Michael and I woke up at my house hours later," I explained to both of them since neither knew this part. "We couldn't remember anything that happened after the first punches were thrown."

"He probably *Dexter*'d you," Dove said.

I managed a laugh. "I thought the same thing."

"Well, it's a good thing I did your job for you then, isn't it?" my father asked.

I had no idea what he was referring to. "What are you talking about?"

Dove practically burst at the seams, her arms flailing, hip jutting out. "You really don't know? Is that why you haven't called me? Or texted me back?"

My body stiffened as confusion wrapped around me like a thick fog. "Someone had better tell me what the fuck is going on right now," I demanded, feeling embarrassed and stupid for being so clueless.

"Your father objected. He stopped the wedding." She waved a hand in his direction.

My world spun in that moment. It tilted, reversed itself, made me dizzy. I had to walk over to the wall and lean against it for balance before trying to catch my breath.

"Wait a second." I held up a finger. "You're not married?"

I wanted to fucking bawl like a baby with the relief. I hadn't even looked at Dove's ring finger. I hadn't wanted to see the extra band there. Couldn't handle it.

"No, you idiot." Dove swatted my shoulder, and my father actually managed to smile. "Once your father objected, it started a wave of objections. It was surreal. The whole church was shouting at once. You should have seen Trevor's face. He stormed out."

"Holy shit," I said in a whisper, still not believing that all this was true.

"Son, we have business to discuss. You can catch up on the details and thank me later," my father said as my heart rate tried to return to normal.

"I need a minute."

Dove was in front of me, her face filled with so much emotion and elation. I read her like a book. She hadn't known I'd tried to stop the wedding. I'd had no idea the wedding hadn't happened. She'd only said yes to Trevor because he had threatened her dad. I figured as much but still needed to hear the truth. Dove would never have betrayed me like that without cause. My heart had always known that, but my head hadn't been so sure. She still loved me.

"Baby," I whispered, and she smiled at me for what felt like the first time in years. When the person you loved was forcefully removed from your life, it was like losing a limb. You didn't ever get over it; you simply lived with the phantom pain. "I love you."

"I only love you," she said before leaping into my arms and wrapping her legs around my waist.

My hands moved to her ass as I held her tight there.

"I'll make this right. I promise," I said before reminding her who she belonged with. My mouth was on hers, claiming her tongue with my own.

I planned on marrying this woman tomorrow if she'd have me. I'd never let anyone or anything come between us again.

"I'm not mad at you anymore," she said.

I kissed her again, stifling a thankful laugh. You never knew with Dove.

My father cleared his throat. "Jesus, you two. Enough. Do this *making up* stuff later. We need to talk."

I looked around once more. "You sure you want to do it here? Should we go somewhere more private?"

He shook his head. "This is better. In public is safer for now."

Safer?

"What the hell is going on?"

My father looked uncomfortable, like Dove had mentioned earlier. It was the first time I'd seen him look like he wasn't the one in control.

"I hate that it's come to this, but I need you to step into the family business."

This. Shit. Again.

It always came back to this. Politics. The family business. My refusal to be a part of it.

"No."

"I'm not asking this time."

Dove reached for my hand, her fingers interlocking with mine, reminding me that I wasn't alone.

"Why do you need me when you have Trevor? Can't he do whatever it is that you need?"

"I thought so, but these people not-so-politely disagreed."

"And why's that?"

"Because Trevor isn't family. They knew that if he was threatened or used as a bargaining tool against me, I wouldn't budge if I didn't want to. I don't care what they do to Trevor, and they know it. He's not my son."

I stood stoic, soaking in all of the information that he had slowly dished out for the first time. Trevor wasn't enough for whoever these people were, and my father was even more of a fuckup than I'd originally thought. None of it made me want to bend to their whim. I'd decided years ago that I'd never turn into the kind of men my father and grandfather were. And I didn't feel any differently about that decision today than when I'd first made it.

"They can still threaten my life and use me against you, no matter what I do for a living."

I tried to make sense of it all. I didn't understand why my existence wasn't enough. It wasn't like my development company didn't wield power in its own right. I could do plenty of illegal things, but I never would, and I was sure they knew that.

Why was me in a political seat suddenly a requirement?

"They can. But getting you into the right position ensures that once I retire, you'll continue the shared legacy that we've created. That legacy includes doing things for this family as they do for us. I need you to carry that on, or who knows what they'll do?"

"I literally have no idea what you're talking about, and I don't care."

This was beyond ridiculous. Some over-the-top dramatic-movie bullshit that couldn't be real or true. Being so far removed from my family and the circles they moved in the past handful of years had kept me in the dark. I liked it that way. Wanted it to stay like that.

"Dominic, I have a contract that only you can fulfill."

"What kind of contract?"

Dove squeezed my hand once more, reminding me that she was by my side and wasn't going anywhere.

I could do anything, stand up to anyone, as long as I still had her next to me.

"One that's been in effect for hundreds of years. It's not a big deal. We simply approve their permits and requests without question or police involvement, and they make sure we're protected and stay in power."

"Protected how?"

"They remove any potential threats, and they assure we get elected to whatever seat we seek. Have you ever known a DeLuca to lose any office they run for?" he asked and waited for me to respond.

I didn't realize it wasn't a rhetorical question.

I thought back over our family history. We'd never lost. At least, not that I was aware or ever told. "No."

"They ensure that we don't."

"Who are we talking about? What other family?" Dove asked that question before I had a chance to.

Only one other family in our town wielded as much power as ours did, but I'd never seen my father so much as acknowledge any of them in public, let alone overheard him talk about them in private.

"The Firenzis," he said, and my blood went cold.

I guessed he did interact with them after all.

The Firenzis were one of the richest families in the county with investments spread across multiple ventures, going back generations. Their wealth had always added up from my perspective, but everyone else in town wholeheartedly disagreed.

Even Dove didn't like them. She'd said that the men in the family always creeped her out, and she knew they were as dirty as everyone claimed. She'd made me promise once when we were just starting our businesses that I'd stay away from them and never get involved with their dealings, no matter what. I trusted her judgment, so of course, I'd told her yes.

The rumor mill had continued to run rampant over the years. Everyone claimed that the Firenzis' various businesses were nothing but fronts for a slew of illegal activities. They were accused of selling drugs and guns and money laundering, but as far as I knew, there was never any proof. If the Firenzis were as bad as people said they were, wouldn't they be rotting away in a jail cell somewhere?

Then, I remembered seeing the whiteboard in Bob Tryst's office and hearing his words. *"Someone's always working that case."*

Dove let out a soft breath before asking, "Is that where my dad comes in?"

My father looked caught off guard. "Your dad? What do you mean?"

I swore Dove's knees almost gave out, and I reached for her just in time to stop her from falling.

"I've got you," I said as I held on to her, but her voice didn't come out.

Her green eyes looked at me, silently pleading for help.

"Trevor said he had information on Bob taking bribes and that he'd have him arrested and thrown in prison." I filled in the blanks, so Dove didn't have to.

"Oh Jesus. Is that how he got you to say yes?" My father sounded almost incredulous. "I always wondered. Trevor never told me the specifics."

I swallowed hard as a gust of wind blew between us, making Dove's hair wrap around her face. "Hold on." I tucked the strands behind her ear, holding them in place. This day kept getting more and more messed up. "Let's back up for a second. Did you plant proposing to Dove in Trevor's head?"

I'd always thought it was my father's idea, orchestrated by him and for his benefit alone. That Trevor never would have had the balls to do something like that without my father's backing.

"Yes," he admitted, and I was actually shocked.

I wasn't sure that he even knew how to tell the truth.

"Once the Firenzis informed me that Trevor wouldn't cut it and that it had to be you going forward, it was the only thing I could think of to do. Trevor didn't need to even be convinced. He was on board the second the idea left my mouth."

I let out a disgusted sound. "Of course, he was. And of course, the first thing you'd think of was how to manipulate me instead of actually communicating with me."

He scoffed. "First of all, I never thought the wedding would actually happen." He focused his attention on Dove. "I had no idea what Trevor said to get you to go along with it, but I was certain Dom"—he looked back at me—"would reach out to me when he heard the news. Then, we'd work out a deal to get Dom into the business, and then the fake engagement between Dove and Trevor would go away, and we'd put it all behind us."

I shifted my weight from foot to foot, taking it all in and letting it simmer until I boiled over. "You could have just talked to me. Told me what was going on. We could have come up with a better plan. One that didn't involve Dove at all!"

"You have no idea what goes on behind closed doors, Dominic. How many people want and need things from me that I'm not capable of giving, but I have to figure out a way to do it anyway. I thought you'd go ballistic when you heard about Dove, but instead of reaching out to yell at me and blame me, you cut me off and went radio silent," he explained before shaking his head and wiping at the spit forming at the corners of his mouth. "I should have seen that one coming. Anyway, I never thought you'd let Dove go through with it, so the threat of her actually marrying Trevor was never real in my mind. But it had to be real in yours. I was using Trevor to get you to do what I needed. What the family needed. But I guess Trevor had his own agenda."

"He just wanted to hurt Dominic and make him suffer," Dove said without any real emotion. "He hates Dom so much. He's fueled by jealousy, envy, and rage. Marrying me so that Dominic couldn't was the beginning and end of his plan."

"So, he *is* as stupid as he looks then," my father said with a bit of a chuckle, but neither Dove nor I were laughing.

"So, this whole thing was just to get my attention? To try to trick me into doing what you wanted me to do and make me feel like I had no choice in the matter?"

The very idea infuriated me. People had been hurt for

no good reason, and it all could have been avoided.

"Yeah. I guess I read you wrong. Or I read Trevor wrong."

My mind instantly busied itself, thinking of ways to fix this mess, that I didn't care about who my father did or didn't read right. "Tell us about Dove's dad," I said, wanting total clarification so I could make my next decision wisely.

My father's features twisted, and he dropped his sunglasses over his eyes. "There's nothing to tell. I tried to get him on the payroll years ago, but he's too righteous and good. Even with your life threatened, Dove. That only worked once. And it was a long time ago."

The time she'd overheard back in high school. Dove and I shared a knowing look before her eyes started to water.

"My dad would let you guys kill me?" she asked, her voice shaking with disbelief.

My father stepped closer to us. "No. He would have eventually caved if kept pushing, but I convinced the Firenzis that we didn't need the chief on our payroll. That it would be too risky to have him anyway, too obvious if someone started asking questions. We just needed one person in the station as an extra precaution, just in case. It really didn't matter who. The Firenzis agreed, and it's worked out fine ever since."

"You protected Dove?" I wanted to believe that so badly, but I wasn't sure that I could.

"I knew you'd never recover if anything bad ever happened to her, son. You'd go off the rails, and I'd never get you back. This was years ago—when I still held out hope that your ambitions toward politics would shift and you'd grow up and see how important it was," he explained before adding, "Now, you don't have a choice."

"I disagree," I said before reaching for Dove's hand and clasping it in mine. "Let's go. All three of us. Now."

"Where?" Dove asked before reading my mind.

She knew exactly where we were headed.

HAVE TO FIX THIS

DOVE

We all piled into Dominic's car. He'd insisted on driving, and I knew why. It would have been too risky to ask his father to follow us. Once he realized where we were going, he most likely would have turned around and bailed. Plus, if the Firenzis were as dangerous as he'd hinted at, we couldn't have his car sitting in front of my dad's house for anyone to see or rat out.

Dominic's car being there wouldn't draw anyone's suspicions. He was always there, apparently even when I wasn't.

"Where are we going?" his father asked from the backseat as we made a left turn onto my street. "Let me out." He must have realized where we were headed.

It was better than going to the police station and

talking to my dad there.

"Father," Dominic said, "this is the only way. I'm not getting into the game, so we need his help, or this is never going to end."

"What if he throws me in prison? Or arrests the Firenzis? You think this will end then? That their family will just stop? This doesn't end, son. It doesn't end with you, or your son, or your grandson."

My stomach turned at the idea of our future kids being wrapped up in something so vile without their choice or knowledge.

"It ends today," Dominic said with force, and I believed him. He hated this as much as I did, maybe even more.

He rolled to a stop at the curb, his usual spot, before shutting the engine off. I'd already texted my dad to let him know we were on our way, bringing a guest, and that we needed his help. I didn't want to put too much in writing in case any of our text messages were eventually subpoenaed. What could I say? I'd watched a lot of cop shows, growing up.

The front door opened, and my dad peered outside,

obviously too curious to wait. I didn't miss the look of surprise on his face as soon as he noticed Dominic's father getting out of the backseat.

"Get inside," my dad instructed before waving us in and shutting the door behind us. "You never know who's watching."

"You sound as paranoid as he does," Dominic said, referring to his father.

"That's because we both know who the real enemy is," my dad added, and I realized that the Firenzis were truly bad news.

"They'll kill us," Dominic's father breathed out, clearly uncomfortable.

"They won't," my dad vehemently disagreed. "The Firenzis don't go around, murdering people, regardless of what everyone here in Hopetown says. Rumors start like a match strike in a pile of dry hay. If it doesn't get watered down, it turns into a blazing inferno of lies that grows and spreads until you have no idea what's true and what isn't."

Dominic's dad looked downright surprised. He'd believed that the Firenzis were capable of murder and had done so in the past, which was why he had taken their physical threats to heart. He'd truly thought Dominic's life was in danger. I honestly couldn't blame him. No one knew the facts when it came to that family, and everything was based on hearsay and old wives' tales that people insisted were true.

"They threaten. They hurt. They might send you to the hospital with a broken rib or two, but they don't tend to cross the line into murder. It's too messy, and they have enough on their plates with their illegal businesses and making sure those run as smooth as possible. So far, they've been able to do just that."

"You're sure?" Dominic's father asked, still unable to believe what he was hearing.

"I'm sure."

"Dad," I said, sounding small, and everyone's eyes shifted toward where I was sitting.

"What is it, sweet pea?"

"I've always wondered about Mom and the accident. She wasn't murdered, right?" I'd never come right out and asked him about it before. I figured the truth was too painful for him to talk about, but since we'd brought up the topic of murder and being murdered, it seemed like the right time.

"Oh, no, sweet pea. She wasn't. It really was an accident. She swerved to avoid hitting a deer and lost control of the car. It was a freak accident. Most people wouldn't have died from the impact alone, but she did. Sometimes, things happen that we have no explanation for. But no one had her killed, I promise you that."

He emphasized the main point that I had asked, giving me a sense of peace I'd never realized how desperately I needed. The rumors had always circulated in the back of my mind and lived there, taking up space. Now, I could finally let them go.

"Thank you."

"Now, tell me what's going on. Why are you three here? Although I don't hate seeing this reunion"—he wagged his finger between Dominic and me with a smile on his face—"at least tell me it means what I think it does."

"It does," Dominic said without needing to further explain.

He and I were back together, where we belonged, and nothing was ever going to change that again.

"One thing before we get started." My dad took a seat at the kitchen table, and we all followed suit. "I never got the chance to thank you for what you did."

He looked directly at Dominic's father, a man I knew he couldn't stand, and extended his hand. The two men shook, and I wondered how many times that had ever happened before today. They gave each other a nod, a silent understanding passing between them that, right here and now, we were all on the same side.

As we sat around the table, answering all my dad's questions and filling in the blanks, my dad actually looked happy. Or maybe it was relieved.

"We've been working on them for years, you know? We've always been missing the one piece that would hold it all together. The glue, so to speak. Otherwise, we knew the case would fall apart during trial."

"What about me?" Dominic's father asked, clearly worried about his own neck.

"We know you've done things like grant them permits, got closed buildings to reopen, and allowed them to have access to multiple inaccessible private properties. But those are all basically misdemeanors on their own. If you testify against them, I can get any potential and future charges against you dropped with no jail time."

"Will I have to give up my office?"

Dominic's dad was always worried about his reputation and prestige. If he had to step down, I knew he would spin it in a way that still made him sound like a good guy who was doing it for all the right reasons even though he wasn't.

"I'm actually not sure. It depends on the deal we cut. If we can't avoid probation, you might have to step down. But you're up for reelection soon, so maybe someone will run against you, and you'll lose the old-fashioned way." My dad stared right at Dominic, and I felt him wince next to me, his grip on my thigh tightening for a second before releasing.

I remembered what his father had told us earlier—that the Firenzis had guaranteed their election win somehow. I wondered how true that really was and if a DeLuca might actually lose without having their help.

"I need to think about it."

"I understand. It's a lot to consider, but don't take too long. This offer isn't on the table indefinitely."

"You don't have anything without me," Dominic's father huffed, and I wanted to smack him for his arrogance.

My dad shrugged like he didn't have a care in the world. "I'll go to trial anyway. Take my chances. And I'll charge you with conspiracy. Prove that you knew all of their dealings and were complicit with every illegal activity they ran through those buildings that you got them the permits for. Every charge might not stick, but I'll get one or two to stand up in court. You'll do jail time. You'll be disgraced. It's all anyone will remember about you."

Damn.

My dad was hard core. I had no idea how much of that was even a possibility or true, but it was enough to scare the confidence right out of Dominic's dad.

"I'll get back to you with my decision in twenty-four hours."

"Sounds good."

"We'd better go," Dominic said abruptly, as if suddenly aware of the severity of our discussion and the potential ramifications heading our way.

"Sweet pea," my dad said before pulling me into a hug,

"you good?"

"I'm great."

"I'm happy for you. One day, you'll fill me in on everything, right?" he asked.

I realized that I still hadn't told him what had happened between me and Trevor—the lies and blackmail. We'd talked on the phone since the failed wedding, but I'd kept to myself for the most part, wallowing in self-pity and staying angry with Dominic for leaving me.

"Yes. I'll explain everything after we get through this," I said, referring to the Firenzis and Dominic's father.

Dominic stepped into our space and threw an arm around me, pressing a kiss to the side of my head. "Sir, I'm going to marry your daughter, if that's okay with you."

I stifled a surprised laugh. Not because of what Dominic had asked, but because of how he had asked it, with me standing right there, his tone all aggressive and unflinching. There was zero chance in hell that my dad would ever tell him no, but Dominic wouldn't have listened if he had.

"It's about damn time," my dad answered with a grin.

He was right. It was time.

OUR FUTURE STARTS NOW

DOMINIC

THE DRIVE BACK into town was awkward and quiet. We'd all said so much at Bob's house that there wasn't much more to add without it coming off preachy or full of pressure. My father knew what he needed to do, what the right thing was, but that didn't mean that he would actually do it. And my lecturing him about it more, adding my proverbial two cents, wouldn't change his mind if it was already made up.

Dove reached across the center console and rested her hand on top of my thigh, her fingers pressing into my skin one at a time, like she was playing the piano. It was like no time had passed between us and we had never been apart. I glanced over and caught her watching me, her eyes softening the way they always had. Michael and Kristina used to joke that we both had heart-eye emoji faces whenever we looked at each other. I never wanted that to change.

I still had a few questions though, things I was dying to ask, but I'd do that once we were alone.

"You good, baby?" Dove's voice filtered through the otherwise silent car, and I reached down for her hand and squeezed it in response.

I was more than good.

"Father—" I eyed him from my mirror.

"Not now," he snapped, but I shook my head.

"I have a question about Trevor."

He pulled the seat belt off of his chest before placing it back, acting like he was uncomfortable back there when I knew it wasn't true. My car was a fucking gem. "What about him?"

"How involved in things is he?"

"You mean, with the Firenzis?" he clarified, and I nodded. "He's not. His hands are clean even though he has been dying to get them dirty."

That didn't surprise me in the slightest—the part about him wanting to do bad things. Trevor thrived in chaos and lived for my father's approval. He would have done anything he'd asked, illegal or not.

"How much does he know?"

Father's face twisted as his head bounced from side to side. "He only knows what he needed to."

"Just answer the fucking question," I scoffed.

This wasn't the time to play games or beat around the bush. Details were key.

"He honestly knows very little. The Firenzis never approved of him, so he's been kept in the dark on that side of things. He knows nothing about what we do or how. He does know that we have someone on payroll at the station, only because he overheard me talking about it once recently, but he doesn't know who it is," he said before his lips smacked shut, making a hissing sound. "I guess he just assumed that person was your dad, Dove."

"Makes sense," I added because it would be the easiest assumption to make, especially considering my and Dove's relationship. Trying to manipulate Bob would be anyone's first option.

I spotted my woman's Range Rover sitting where she'd parked it earlier, and I pulled up next to it.

"See you at home?" she asked, her tone unsure, and I leaned across the car and gave her a kiss.

"Or else I'm coming to find you."

She grinned with my mock threat before opening her door and stepping out. We had a lot of making up to do.

"I'll talk to you later, son." My father moved to exit the car as well, but I reached for his arm, stopping him.

He leaned back in, his tired eyes meeting mine with quiet resignation.

"I know you'll do the right thing," was all I said before letting go of his sleeve.

The look on his face actually reassured me, and for once in my life, I believed that he would. Maybe we could mend fences and attempt to have a relationship after all.

I'D GOTTEN BACK home before Dove, so I went to work, straightening out the mess that I'd made in her absence. The kitchen was a bit of a disaster, and I knew she'd be upset if she walked in and saw it that way. I moved the dirty dishes from the sink into the dishwasher, opened a window to let in some fresh air, and raced around the house, lighting every candle we owned.

There was very little that I'd changed or even moved around since she'd left all those months ago. Our bedroom was exactly the same, her things still where she'd last put them. Her face cream was still on the bathroom counter, the top sitting next to it. I was sure it had dried out and wasn't usable anymore, but I'd refused to throw out anything that was once hers. It'd felt like giving up. And that was something I hadn't been willing to do.

Walking into the closet, I scooted my jeans out of the way to reveal a small safe screwed into the back wall. Spinning the dials until I heard the familiar click, I opened the door and pulled out the ring box I'd kept in there for years. Why I'd never proposed was beyond me now that I sat there, thinking about it. I'd made so many excuses as to why we were in no rush, acting like our businesses were more important than our love or that we didn't need to be married until we were ready to have kids. It had been stupid to act like we had all the time in the world to become man and wife when time was the one thing that was never guaranteed.

No one was promised a tomorrow. We all just naively

assumed we'd get one.

A door slammed closed, and I walked to the window and glanced out of it. Dove was pulling clothes on hangars out of the backseat and a suitcase from her trunk. She must have gone to her place to grab at least some of her things. Hiding the ring between two pairs of jeans, I hustled downstairs to go help.

When I reached the front door, she was already opening it, a giant smile on her face.

"Honey, I'm home," she shouted before noticing me rushing toward her. "Oops. Hi."

"You're never leaving again." I reached for her body and lifted it into my arms, devouring her mouth with mine, touching every gentle slope and muscle of her ass in those jeans.

If someone tried to take her from me again, they'd have to pry her from my dead arms.

"I have some more stuff in the car," she said, her eyes still closed from our contact.

"I'll go get it." I turned and watched her bound up the stairs with a handful of her things, knowing that she was back for good.

I brought the last of her things into our bedroom and sat on the edge of the bed, watching her unpack. Excited nerves fluttered through my stomach at the sight.

"You left everything the same." She sounded so sad as she said it, like the realization hurt her somehow.

"What was I supposed to do?"

A small laugh escaped her. "Figured you might burn it all."

"I could never do that."

"I know." She walked to where I was and fell to her knees.

Her head rested on my leg, and I ran my fingers through her long blonde hair.

She looked up at me, her green eyes filled with emotion. "I love you, Dominic. I'm so sorry I couldn't tell you what was going on."

This was the moment. Where the air was finally cleared and all of our mutual questions were answered.

"Can we talk about it?" I asked, helping her to a stand.

"Of course."

We kicked off our shoes and faced each other on the bed, both bracing for what was to come, what secrets would be revealed. I'd already decided that no matter what she told me about Trevor, I'd forgive her.

It was Trevor I'd never forgive.

Dove filled me in on exactly how he'd blackmailed her by using the love she had for her dad against her. He knew that she'd do anything to keep her dad from going to prison, and that fear alone motivated her to go along with his demands. He did the same thing when it came to me, forcing her to stay away. She'd believed that he had information that could hurt me, and Dove would do anything to stop that from happening. I understood completely because if the roles had been reversed, I would have done what she had too.

And even though it was my father's idea, Trevor had apparently reveled in stealing her away from me. She said that his sole focus was to make sure I never touched her again, knowing how much that alone would destroy me from the inside out. Anytime they could be photographed together for the press, he took full advantage, wrapping a possessive arm around her waist, holding her tightly against him. Knowing that I would see the pictures fueled him. I had known the guy hated me, but I'd never realized just how much. And honestly, I didn't get why.

"He never tried to sleep with you?" I cringed inwardly as I asked this question even though she'd already told me that they'd never done more than kiss on the cheek.

It was the one thing that burned holes in my mind. The thought of him even touching her made me see red. I wasn't sure what I would do if he had actually forced her to have sex with him. Probably rip him from limb to limb and feed him to some lions somewhere. Or leave the pieces to rot. No dignity in life was equal to no dignity in death.

"No." She shook her head, reassuring me. "The whole situation was weird. He let me stay in my own place, and he only required me to attend certain public events with him. Otherwise, we barely even talked when we were at home. But he always knew what I was doing and who I was with. I never felt safe. And I was always worried that if I got out of line, he'd have my dad arrested. I lived every day in some level of fear, always looking over my shoulder."

I pushed off the bed and walked to the side she was on and took her in my arms. I'd never let anyone hurt her again. "I'm so sorry you went through that."

I was sorry that my woman had been emotionally tortured for months, but I was also pissed the hell off and wanted revenge.

"I'll make him pay," I growled, half-expecting her to tell me not to.

"I know you will," was what she said instead, and we both grinned.

ALWAYS & FOREVER

DOVE

"BABY," DOMINIC SAID with a grin, "I'll be right back." He disappeared into the closet we shared before returning just as quickly and falling to one knee on the ground in front of me.

"What are you doing?" I asked, my mouth falling open.

He held a ring between three fingers, but I focused on his face and the words he was saying instead. Who cared about a piece of jewelry when the man I loved was asking me the most important question of my life?

"Dove, I always knew I couldn't live without you, but I never understood just how vital you were to my existence until now. The pain I felt, knowing that you were no longer mine ..." He sucked in a ragged breath. "I don't know how to put it into words, baby, but it's not something I ever want to feel again. I won't make it through. Not without you. You are my literal everything. I have nothing if I don't have you. And I refuse to live another day without you as my wife. I promise to never let anyone or anything come between us again. I'll hunt down anyone who tries to hurt you and make them pay. As long as I live, I promise you that. You'll never have to look over your shoulder again. I will protect you. Keep you safe. Marry me, Dove. Tell me you forgive me and be my wife."

Tears trickled down my strong man's face, and it was as unnerving as it was sexy. I knew that I was the only person on earth who got to see Dominic vulnerable, and I liked it that way. No one else deserved to witness this side of him.

"Forgive you?" I repeated. "There's nothing to forgive. Of course I'll marry you."

"Today?" he asked, excited.

I laughed and looked at the digital clock on the nightstand. It was already after five. The courthouse would be closed.

"Tomorrow," I said.

He finally put the ring on my finger, and I got a good look at it. The deep blue sapphire, surrounded by diamonds, made my eyes water.

"My mom's birthstone," I said softly.

"You always said that's what you wanted," he explained. "But if you don't like it, I'll buy you something else."

"No. It's perfect. I love it." I looked at him through my hazy vision. "I love you."

"I love you too, baby. I wasn't kidding about getting married tomorrow."

"I know you weren't." I grinned. "I don't want to wait either. I don't want a big wedding. Just us."

"And your dad," he added.

And I could not have loved this man any more than I did in this moment. He knew what I needed before I did, and he was always so damn thoughtful.

I nodded, and he reached for the hem of my shirt before pulling it off and rising from his kneeling position.

"It's been too long since I've touched you." He ran his fingertips down the side of my rib cage before moving to unclasp my bra and tossing it somewhere.

I shivered in response.

"It's been too many days since I've tasted you," he said.

I knew what was coming next. Craved it like I needed it to survive.

When he pulled my jeans from my body, his breath caught, and I knew I'd never get tired of the way he reacted to seeing me exposed. I helped remove my thong, revealing myself to him, and his eyes grew wide as he stared at me like I was a pot of gold at the end of a rainbow.

"Mine," he growled before diving in headfirst.

Holy shit.

It had been too long since this man's tongue was in me, tasting me, fucking me just the way I liked. He ate me slowly at first, devouring every drop like it might be his last, and I threw my head back with the pleasure it elicited. Reaching for his hair, I pulled at it, my nails scratching his scalp.

"Oh God, don't stop," I breathed out as I collapsed fully on my back on the bed.

Dominic reached for my thighs and tugged me lower.

"You taste so fucking good, baby. I've missed this," he said, and I felt myself blush with his admission.

There had been more than a few times during our separation when I thought I'd never have this again. Or when I believed that it would be years before we'd be able to make our way back to one another. This was better than I ever could have imagined.

My thighs clenched around his head, and my hips started to buck against his mouth. He started eating me more furiously, his tongue fucking and lapping with reckless abandon. I was so close to coming undone, and he knew it. He didn't stop his pace, and I might have killed him if he tried.

"Dominic," I said between labored breaths, "I'm coming."

"I know." His answer was hot against me, but he still didn't stop. My man was a multitasker.

My body convulsed, the orgasm spreading throughout me. I shook and tried to push his head away, but he refused. His tongue still licked as I came, eating every last drop that I gave him before he finally relented.

He looked so damn satisfied and smug.

"Get in me," I demanded as he stripped out of his own clothes, and I lay there, wide-eyed, drinking every inch of him in.

That man had been made for me, and I couldn't imagine a day when I'd ever not want him.

"Yes, ma'am." He saluted before taking his hard length in his hand and guiding it toward my entrance.

I held my breath and lifted my hips for him. He teased me with the tip before plunging inside, filling me up entirely. I gasped at the suddenness of it before relaxing.

How had I lived without having him inside me?

"You feel amazing." I reached for his back and pulled him harder against me, my nails digging into his flesh, letting him know that I wanted it rougher, stronger. It was the silent cue I always gave him to not hold back.

"You don't want it sweet, baby?" he asked.

I looked at the ring on my finger before shaking my head. "Take what's yours."

I wanted to be owned.

Claimed.

Dominated.

I needed to be reminded about who I belonged to, and Dominic needed the same, whether he realized it or not.

He was mine. And I was his.

And nothing would ever change that again.

He pinned my arms above my head, holding them so tight that I couldn't move out of his grasp if I tried. He fucked me, his erect cock moving in and out with such force that I thought we might break the headboard. When he grabbed one of my legs and tossed it over his shoulder, I considered screaming with pleasure at the angle he was now reaching. He gripped my inner thigh, his body plunging into me over and over again, and still … I wanted more.

"Fuck me, baby. Fuck me harder," I cried out, and he went to work, sweat beading on his chest and brow.

He threw my leg off his shoulder and pinned it to my side. His face twisted as he started fucking me that way, and I knew he was going to come.

"Just like that, baby. Come in me," I begged, wanting every last drop from his dick inside me.

"Fuck," he cried out. "I love you so much," he said before leaning down and pressing a kiss to my mouth.

Our tongues touched, and the kiss was frantic, messy. He pulled away before I was ready and fucked me so hard that I thought I might walk crooked for the next week.

"Tell me you love me, Dove. Tell me it's only me," he demanded, and I gave him what he craved.

"Only you, baby. Always and forever. I'll only love you," I said.

As the last words left my mouth, he shuddered and exploded inside of me. There was nothing that turned me on more than the feeling of him losing himself inside my body. I took it all, clenching around his cock, and refused to let him exit until he was done convulsing.

He collapsed on top of me, his heartbeat pounding through his sweaty chest. Our bodies still connected at the pelvis.

"Tomorrow," he breathed out.

Then, I swore I heard him snore.

Men. Give them sex, and they slept like babies.

I WOKE UP the next morning, fear and paranoia greeting me in full force, the way it had each day since the blackmail had started. I never fully realized just how accustomed I'd grown to my previous situation until the moment that I sat in bed, reminding myself over and over again that the horrors from the past were done. I didn't have to worry about Trevor or my dad going to jail ever again. And I was back where I belonged … with Dominic.

Glancing to my right, I saw that he was still sleeping, a peaceful look on his face. He was so handsome that I was tempted to take a picture. Looking down at my left hand, I found myself smiling. The ring was delicate and intricate yet still absolutely breathtaking. It was so much softer than I could ever be.

Reaching for my phone, I pulled it free from the charger and started an internet search. I wasn't sure what we needed to get married at the courthouse, so I looked it up. The biggest hiccup seemed to be acquiring a marriage license, so I fired off an email to ask how long that would take and for their earliest reservation. Dominic and I knew everyone who worked there, so I was certain that we could pull some strings if need be.

The bed moved, and I turned to see Dominic staring at me, like I might not be real. His fingers brushed across my cheek.

"You're really here," he said, his voice groggy. "What are you doing?"

"Looking up wedding stuff," I answered, and that woke him right up.

He pushed the pillow behind his back and sat up straight. "Tell me what I need to do."

DOMINIC AND I stood in a room with a judge, my dad, Michael, and Kristina. I had an ivory dress I'd fallen in love with hanging in my closet for years, so I wore that now. It was form-fitting, flattering, and way too short. I wasn't sure I could even bend over in it without showing everyone my ass, so I stood tall.

I'd gone to the jewelry store with Kristina and bought a ring for Dominic and a small band for myself. There was no way I was letting him walk around town without a ring on his wedding finger after today. I wanted everyone to know that he was finally legally mine.

We exchanged vows and wedding bands, and then it was over as quickly as it had begun. No one objected when they were asked. And everyone cried. Even my dad. It was perfect—intimate, private, and romantic. I'd realized that I didn't need any of the usual fanfare to celebrate our union. I only needed my husband.

And now, I had him. For better or worse. In sickness and in health. Till death did us part. And then we promised to find each other in the next life.

JUSTICE

DOMINIC

TWO MONTHS LATER

When all was said and done, the Firenzis takedown had been a success. It was far more convoluted than anyone could have known, but the right people were now behind bars, awaiting a trial that would take years to come to fruition. None of us were certain that they'd stay alive for that long. Crazy shit happened to criminals once they were inside a prison cell. Your past tended to catch up with you in there, and vendettas no longer went unanswered.

My father had actually agreed to testify, which surprised and impressed me, but when it came down to it, Bob didn't need him after all. He'd taken his statement, which included coercion and threats to life, but in the end, two of the Firenzi family members spoke up and were willing to do the takedown themselves. They said it was their "duty" to put a stop to the vicious cycle that had gone on for too long, and they didn't want anyone else getting wrapped up in their dirty laundry.

Apparently, they had been wanting out of the business for as long as they'd been in it, but they had no idea how to leave. They felt trapped with no way out. It was a feeling I understood and could relate to intimately, only I'd been able to tell my old man no and walk away. It wasn't the same in their family. There was no choice. There would be no walking away.

It was a shocking turn of events, and the entire town was rattled when the news slowly started coming out. The Firenzi family had been shunned by the community for so long that welcoming them back into the fold felt incredibly uncomfortable for most, if not impossible.

Dove and I tried to help in our own way. She took the two of them on as clients, sold their family home, and helped them buy new ones within the town limits, proving that they could be trusted and not feared. It also showed the townspeople that the two remaining Firenzis wanted to be part of our community and not ostracized anymore.

I gave them both jobs working at my company. I actually became close with the youngest Firenzi son, Jacobi, who was only five years older than I was. And even though I liked him a lot, giving him a job had been my way of keeping an eye on his family at first.

Initially, we had all feared some sort of backlash, actually waited for a slew of Firenzis from all over the country to fly in and get their revenge on everyone in town, but it never came. That didn't mean that it never would, but Jacobi made it sound like the most vicious of the Firenzis were dying out. It seemed like the older generations would soon be extinct, and the younger ones were ready to usher in a new way of life. One that didn't involve putting their family in harm's way at every turn.

Jacobi had actually been grateful for the arrests, although he'd deny it vehemently if ever asked.

As for Trevor, well, he'd tried to become a ghost of sorts. Disappeared soon after the failed wedding, too humiliated to continue living in town after so many had spoken up against him. His ego couldn't handle facing anyone after that. I knew where he was at all times—I had a private investigator keeping tabs on him. When I was ready to make him pay for what he'd done to the people I loved, I'd know exactly where to find him.

I pulled into the driveway of our house, cut off the engine, and grinned at the sight of my wife's Range Rover. I'd never get tired of seeing it there. If I ever started taking her or her presence for granted, I'd just remember what it'd felt like to lose her, and that feeling would disappear instantly.

When I walked through the front door, the smell of sugar and chocolate hit my senses. "Wife!" I shouted.

Dove appeared out of nowhere, wearing nothing but a see-through black bra and panty set.

"I baked," she said with a half-grin.

I started salivating at the sight of her, my eyes locked on her full tits, my dick waking up to greet her.

"Uh-huh." I always turned stupid whenever I saw her naked. The woman was a dream.

She laughed. "I said, I baked." She pointed at the tray of cookies on the counter, clearly hinting at something that I wasn't quite getting.

"You think I care about cookies when you look like

that?"

"Go look at what else I made for you." She pointed at the counter.

Even though I had no idea what she was up to, I did as she'd asked. Because I always would. Because that woman owned me and I didn't care who knew.

Stepping toward the kitchen island, I saw what looked like a rectangular watch box sitting next to the tray of chocolate cookies. "What's this?" I asked before looking over my shoulder, wondering if she'd bought me a gift and why. As long as she was mine, I didn't need anything else.

"Open it."

Removing the top, I looked inside, seeing some sort of unfamiliar contraption.

"Read it," she instructed.

PREGNANT.

Holy shit.

I spun around, searching for my beautiful, magical wife. "We're pregnant?"

"We're pregnant," she repeated, her green eyes watering with the words.

"You made me a baby," I practically purred. "Is that why you baked?" It was a stupid question, but it was the first thing I'd thought of. Dove wasn't typically a baker.

"The cravings are real, baby daddy. Already. Give me all the chocolate," she said, licking her fingers, and I was instantly hard again.

"I'll build you a fucking house made out of it," I said before reaching for her body and kissing her senseless.

She tasted like sugar and cocoa, and I wanted to eat her up from head to toe. Literally.

"You know how they say being pregnant makes you horny?" she whispered against my ear, and I wondered if it was a trick question or not. I must have taken too long to respond because she answered for me. "Well, it's true. So horny. All the time. Take me upstairs. Now."

She turned to walk away, and I was set to follow her perfect ass, but she turned around, pointing, "Bring the cookies!"

And I grabbed the whole damn tray.

EPILOGUE

DOVE

FIVE YEARS LATER

IT WAS OUR sweet girl, Willow's, fourth birthday today. How had four years flown by so quickly? I could barely remember all the sleepless nights and dirty diapers; they seemed so long ago now. Next year, she'd be starting "big-girl school," as she called it. Some days, I couldn't believe it. Where had the time gone?

I stood in our beautiful backyard with decorations hanging from every tree, watching my husband jump in a horse-themed bouncy house with our daughter. She was laughing, her straight brown hair flying all around her with each jump. Dominic was smiling, too, his hands holding both of hers as they hopped together before falling dramatically to the inflated floor before getting up and doing it all over again.

"How are you holding up, sweet pea?" my dad asked as he wrapped an arm around my middle and gave me a side hug.

He knew that I'd been planning every detail of this party for months. No one had ever told me that being a mom was so tiring and downright stressful. I constantly second-guessed everything I did and felt like nothing was ever good enough.

"I'm just happy today is finally here and that Willow loves it. You should have seen her face this morning. She was so surprised. How's work?"

I looked at him, grateful that the tiredness he'd worn the past few years seemed to be wearing off. He actually looked well rested and healthier than I'd seen him in a long time.

"Calm," he said before giving me a grateful look. "It's bizarre."

A small laugh escaped from my lips. I understood the feeling completely. There had been so much chaos in town after the Firenzi arrests that the peace that followed the end of the trial was unnerving. It was almost like we didn't know how to function in serenity anymore, but trust me, we were all trying.

I glanced across the yard toward the chairs positioned underneath one of our trees in the shade. Dominic's mother and father both sat there, looking relaxed as they sipped on wine. They were watching Willow and Dominic jump, too, smiles on both of their faces.

The fences between us weren't completely mended, but everyone was truly trying. Dominic's father had retired, claiming that it was time to focus on his family needs instead of the town. And his mother embraced their newfound life, finally free of obligation and constant scrutiny as a politician's wife. I never expected such a drastic change from her. She'd always come across so cold and calculating to me in the past, but I guessed I'd never really known her. She was much kinder than I remembered. And I found myself enjoying the time we spent together.

"Hey! We're here!" Kristina's voice rang out as she walked into my backyard, holding hands with her boyfriend, Jacobi Firenzi, and a massively wrapped present for Willow.

She and Jacobi had been together for years now, and I couldn't have been happier for her. He'd turned out to be a really good guy who had gotten a bad rap simply because of his last name. But now, everyone in Hopetown seemed to love him.

I directed Kristina to the gift table and then gave them both hugs before my incredibly sweaty husband appeared at my side, his lips pressing against my temple.

"I need to talk to you," he whispered, and I got a little nervous at how serious his voice sounded.

"Mommy." Willow was right behind Dominic, on his heels.

I should have known. She followed him everywhere. Any other girl would have made me jealous, but not this one. The way she loved him only made me love him more.

"Hey, baby girl. How's the bouncy house?" I asked, moving her sweat-filled hair out of her face and tucking the strands behind her ears.

"I want Pops to jump with me." She reached for my dad's hand, and he gave me a concerned look.

"I'm not sure bouncy houses are good for Pops," I tried to explain before leaning down closer to her. I whispered loud enough for everyone around us to hear, "He might break a leg or something."

Her dark eyes grew super wide. "Really?" She dropped his hand. "I don't want you to break a leg, Pops," she said before whipping her head toward Jacobi. "Uncle Jobi, I bet you won't break anything. Come jump with me!"

Jacobi reached down and started untying his laces. "Race you," he said before Willow took off running toward the house, her giggle echoing in the air. Jacobi was hot on her track.

"I think you've lost him," I said to Kristina, knowing that anytime he was around Willow, she stole all of his attention.

"You're going to have to give him one of your own," Dominic added with a grin.

Kristina swatted his shoulder. "We're not even married yet. Or engaged. Tell him to hurry up and ask already."

She pouted, and I knew in that moment that Dominic would talk to Jacobi, and we'd have a wedding to attend sooner rather than later. My man was good that way.

"Baby," Dominic said in my ear before squeezing my hand, reminding me that we apparently needed to talk.

"I guess we'll be right back," I said, excusing myself from everyone as they rolled their eyes, most likely assuming that he and I were sneaking off to make out somewhere. I couldn't really blame them, considering the fact that we did just that more often than not during parties.

My husband held on to my hand and pulled me inside our house and upstairs to our bedroom, where he closed the door behind us.

"You're scaring me," I blurted out as soon as we stopped moving.

"I just got some news. It couldn't wait," he said, holding up his cell phone.

My throat constricted. "What is it?" I couldn't even begin to process what this might be about.

The Firenzis were in prison and would spend the rest of their lives there. As far as I knew, we weren't blamed for their takedown, not even Dominic's father, so no one was out to get us.

"Trevor," Dominic said.

That one word made my world spin and threw me back in time so quickly that I thought I might lose my balance.

"Is he here?"

I knew how badly Dominic had wanted to seek him out and make him pay for what he'd done to me at first. But the more time that passed, chasing him down and getting revenge seemed less and less important. And once we found out I was pregnant with Willow, everything changed.

Trevor was no longer a priority in our life. Revenge seemed almost pointless. Protecting me and Willow became Dominic's only goal. He was going to be a dad, and he didn't take that responsibility lightly. We had a long conversation about it all one night, where I not only gave him permission, but also downright insisted that he let the vendetta against Trevor go. It wasn't worth it.

Not anymore.

And plus, we'd won. Dominic and I had gotten married and pregnant, and we were completely in love.

Trevor hadn't even been a blip on our radar. Not when we had something more important growing inside of me.

Dominic held me in his arms and led me to the bed, where we both sat down. "He's dead."

I hadn't expected that. "He's dead?" I repeated.

"How?"

"Apparently, he pissed off the wrong people. He got knifed in a bar last night. Didn't make it through surgery."

"How'd you find out?"

"I had him followed. Just so I always knew where he was or if he tried to come back here," he explained.

When I thought that I might be upset by Dominic's actions, I realized that I was actually grateful for them.

"I never wanted to be caught off-guard. If Trevor planned on coming back to Hopetown, I wanted to be ready for him."

"I can't believe he's dead."

I felt nothing. I'd expected to feel at least some measure of relief, but he didn't have that kind of hold over me anymore. I'd stopped fearing him a long time ago. Because I had Dominic. The man who would never let anything happen to me or his daughter.

"Are you okay?" he asked.

I leaned over, pressing my mouth to his, my tongue moving inside slowly, before pulling away. "I'm perfect. You?"

"Ready to celebrate," he said before hopping down and

helping me to my feet. "This is a great day."

He was so elated with the news, and honestly, I couldn't blame him at all.

"I love you, baby."

"I love you too."

"You know I'd never let anything happen to my girls."

"I know."

When we started walking down the stairs and toward the backyard, I remembered that someone was still missing.

"Where the heck is Michael?" I stopped moving. "If he doesn't show up, Willow might never forgive him."

Dominic grinned. "Oh, he's coming. He just had to stop and pick something up first."

"What are you guys up to?" I shook my head because whenever Dominic wanted to do something too over the top for our little girl, he just told Michael to do it instead. He thought it would keep him out of trouble that way.

"Nothing." He kissed my lips before we walked out the sliding back door and rejoined the party.

I watched as he sprinted back toward the bounce house, anxious to get back in.

"Everything okay?" Kristina sidled up next to me while her boyfriend was still being held hostage by my daughter.

"Trevor's dead," I said, and her mouth dropped open.

"Hall-e-freaking-lujah!" she shouted, thrusting a fist in the air, and everyone looked at us.

Avoiding their questioning glances, I glanced around the yard instead and saw Michael walking in, his right arm holding some sort of rope behind him.

"I'm going to kill them both," I growled, and Kristina whipped her head around before she bent in half and started laughing hysterically. "I'm going to kill you too," I said, mentally adding her name to the growing list in my head.

"A pony? He got her a freaking pony?!" she said through her laughter, and my eyes found Dominic's instantly.

He simply offered me a nonchalant shrug, as if he'd had no knowledge of what Michael had done. As if this whole thing hadn't been his idea in the first place, when I knew that it definitely was. I bet if I checked our credit card statement, I'd see the purchase on there, paid for in full by him.

“The best uncle in the world is here,” Michael shouted into the crowd before I heard Willow’s muffled scream.

“Is that for me?” She came bounding out of the bounce house, sprinting toward Michael before she thought better of it and slowed to a walk. “I don’t want to scare her. Oh, she’s so pretty. Is she a girl? Is she for me, Uncle Michael?” Her head swung around, searching for her dad. “Daddy, is she mine?”

“Don’t ask your dad. Ask me. The best uncle in the whole world. I’m the one who brought her. Me. Your favorite uncle. The best guy on the planet. Hello!”

Michael was ridiculous, and even when I wanted to smack him, I still wanted to hug him. He was that lovable. Willow jumped into his arms before saying something in his ear that none of us could hear, but Michael started cracking up. He whispered back, and the look on Willow’s face told me everything I needed to know.

We were now the owners of a freaking real-life pony.

“Don’t be mad.” Dominic appeared at my side and kissed my neck sweetly.

“Don’t distract me with your kisses.” I pretended to be

upset, but I really wasn't. I just didn't want it living in our backyard.

"Before you ask, she has a stall at the stables," he said, as if reading my mind.

"You just think of everything, don't you, Mr. DeLuca?" I asked in a sassy tone.

"I do," he sassed back.

"So, what are you thinking of next?" I turned around to face him, my body pressed so tight against his that I could feel him growing harder against me.

"I think I'm going to put another baby in you."

"What are you waiting for then?" I asked with a challenging grin before I sprinted toward the door and caught sight of him right at my back.

We'd fill this whole town with little DeLucas, and I was going to love every second of it.

THE END

Thank you so much for reading Dove and Dominic's story! I was OBSESSED with this book, and I hope you loved it as much as I did.

I wrote the Fun for the Holidays collection of stories to give you sexy, quick, lighthearted reads that you could get lost in and enjoy. I hope you're loving them. They made writing fun again!

Did you miss the last story—Spring's Second Chance? You can read it everywhere now. Get ready to fall in love with a professional surfer on Oahu's North Shore!

And don't forget to grab the next one in the series—Summer Lovin'—which is out on all retailers now!

Preorder August's book—Flirting with Sunshine—so you don't miss it when it releases on August 1!

Other Books by J. Sterling

Bitter Rivals—an enemies-to-lovers romance
Dear Heart, I Hate You
In Dreams—a new adult college romance
Chance Encounters—a coming-of-age story

THE GAME SERIES
The Perfect Game—Book One
The Game Changer—Book Two
The Sweetest Game—Book Three
The Other Game (Dean Carter)—Book Four

THE PLAYBOY SERIAL
Avoiding the Playboy—Episode #1
Resisting the Playboy—Episode #2
Wanting the Playboy—Episode #3

THE CELEBRITY SERIES
Seeing Stars—Madison & Walker
Breaking Stars—Paige & Tatum
Losing Stars—Quinn & Ryson

THE FISHER BROTHERS SERIES
No Bad Days—a new adult, second-chance romance
Guy Hater—an emotional love story

Adios Pantalones—a single-mom romance

Happy Ending

THE BOYS OF BASEBALL

(THE NEXT GENERATION OF FULLTON STATE BASEBALL PLAYERS)

The Ninth Inning—Cole Anders

Behind the Plate—Chance Carter

Safe at First—Mac Davies

FUN FOR THE HOLIDAYS

(A COLLECTION OF STAND-ALONE NOVELS WITH HOLIDAY-BASED THEMES)

Kissing My Coworker

Dumped for Valentine's

My Week with the Prince

Fools in Love

Spring's Second Chance

Don't Marry Him

Summer Lovin'

Soaring Through August

Falling for the Boss

Tricked by My Ex

The Thanksgiving Hookup

Christmas with Saint

About the Author

Jenn Sterling is a Southern California native who loves writing stories from the heart. Every story she tells has pieces of her truth in it as well as her life experience. She has her bachelor's degree in radio/TV/film and has worked in the entertainment industry the majority of her life.

Jenn loves hearing from her readers and can be found online at:

Blog & Website:

www.j-sterling.com

Twitter:

www.twitter.com/AuthorJSterling

Facebook:

www.facebook.com/AuthorJSterling

Instagram:

@AuthorJSterling

If you enjoyed this book, please consider writing a spoiler-free review on the site from which you purchased it. And thank you so much for helping me spread the word about my books and for allowing me to continue telling the stories I love to tell. I appreciate you so much. :)

Thank you for purchasing this book.

Sign up for my newsletter to get emails about new releases, upcoming releases, and special price promotions:

NEWSLETTER

Come join my private reader group on Facebook for giveaways:

PRIVATE READER GROUP

facebook.com/groups/ThePerfectGameChangerGroup

Made in United States
North Haven, CT
22 June 2023

38072013R00114